# THE UNTOUCHABLE BROTHER

Wreck My Heart Series Book Two

## LINDSEY POWELL

Content copyright © Lindsey Powell 2022
Cover design by Wicked Dreams Publishing

All rights reserved. No part of this book may be reproduced or utilised in any form, or by any electronic or mechanical means, without the prior written permission of the author.

The characters and events portrayed in this book are fictional. Any similarities to other fictional workings, or real persons (living or dead), names, places, and companies is purely coincidental and not intended by the author.

The right of Lindsey Powell to be identified as the author of this work has been asserted by her in accordance with the Copyright, Designs and Patents act 1988.

A CIP record of this book is available from the British Library.

Except for the original material written by the author, all mention of films, television shows and songs, song titles, and lyrics mentioned in the novel, The Untouchable Brother, are the property of the songwriters and copyright holders.

# Books by Lindsey Powell

## The Perfect Series

Perfect Stranger

Perfect Memories

Perfect Disaster

Perfect Beginnings

The Complete Perfect Series

## Part of Me Series

Part of Me

Part of You

Part of Us

Part of Me: Complete Series

## Control Duet

Losing Control

Taking Control

## Games We Play Series

Checkmate

Poker Face

Dark Roulette

A Valentine Christmas

End Game: A Valentine Wedding

Games We Play Complete Series

## Wreck My Heart Series

Wrecking Ball

The Untouchable Brother

## Stand-alone

Take Me

Fixation

Don't Look Back

## Chapter One

### Zoey

Sitting on the beach and looking at the waves rippling softly, I remind myself how lucky I am.

I'm living a dream life in idyllic surroundings, and the beach just so happens to be my back garden.

Living on a beautiful island, away from all the chaos of my previous life has been wonderful. I had been looking for an escape, a place where no one knew who I was or who my brother was.

You see, my brother is Nate Knowles, notorious crime lord who ran the streets for a long time. It was in his blood, and he had taken over when our parents had been killed years before. It was all he knew, until Kat Wiltshire—now Knowles— walked into his life. She turned his head away from what he knew and showed him what it was like to love hard and to put that one person above anything else.

I am so thankful that Kat came into our lives, because if

she hadn't, then I don't know what my brother would be like now. I mean, he was ruthless back then, but with time, I'm sure he would have become even harder, if that was at all possible.

Kat is my best friend and the sister I never had. Once we met, it was like we just clicked, and our bond is so strong that nothing could break it. She's my family, and not only does she make my brother happy, but she has given me the most beautiful niece to love and cherish. In fact, I can hear her squeals of laughter from where I sit, and it makes me smile as I close my eyes and appreciate the fact that I am still alive.

When we came here five years ago, it was just for a holiday, but Nate quickly made a dream a reality when he bought a house out here and said that it was our home.

It was the escape I had been looking for.

A way out of the life I left behind.

The grief and the guilt that plagued me has taken years to push to the back of my mind, but the death and destruction that we left behind still leaves me with guilt to this day, hidden in my subconscious.

I lost someone that I could really have fallen for. Someone who made me feel alive and wanted, cherished but would give me a run for my money at the same time. Jason Jones is the biker that I lost, the man that died helping me. And I don't know if I will ever truly forgive myself for asking him and some of his crew to help on that fateful day…

*I was so confident when I walked in here. I had a plan, a way to deal with the problem that had been fucking with Nate and Kat for weeks—possibly months, I'm not entirely sure, because my brother kept me out of the loop. I know he always thinks he's protecting me, but I'm a big girl who can roll with the best of them.*

Sure, I may seem like more of a party girl, but underneath, I can be cold-hearted too.

But then I guess that's what big brothers are for—to protect their younger siblings and take the brunt of any danger that comes their way.

Nate being a crime lord meant that he had to always be on his game, on top form, ready to strike down anyone that threatened him or anyone he cared about.

That had only ever been me until Kat came along, and now she's here with me, chained to the wall like a fucking animal whilst the enemy stares at us from across the room.

Motherfucking Jessica.

A woman who Nate trusted and who has totally stabbed him in the back.

"Zoey," Jessica says, as if this is a friendly meet. "What a surprise." Ugh, I always did hate her fucking voice. So whiny and high-pitched. How the hell Nate kept her around, I'll never know—other than maybe feeling sorry for her, I can't see the pull. But then, he did find some guy kicking the shit out of her outside the strip club she used to work in years ago, so maybe he did show the heart that he buries deep down inside on that particular night.

"Quite," I reply deadpan. Other than sticking a knife in this bitch, I want nothing to do with her.

"So, to what do I owe the pleasure of this visit?" she says, standing there, thinking she's lady fucking muck with her arms crossed over her chest and a smirk across her face.

"Oh, you know, just thought it would be good to catch up," I tell her, the sarcasm clear in my voice. And then she laughs, and it makes me cringe. Ugh. I hate everything about her.

"Don't tell me you miss me?" she asks, and I lose any patience I may have been harbouring.

"Cut the bullshit, Jessica. We both know I came here to end you," I snarl at her.

"And you brought along a treat," she says as she turns her attention to Kat. She stalks forward, and I take a moment to appreciate just how different the two women are.

Jessica has short blonde hair and dark grey eyes which are almost squinty, like she's got the sun glaring at her constantly, whereas Kat has long brunette hair and beautiful blue eyes that—usually—sparkle with happiness and mischief. It's why we clicked so well, because I can see a rebellious spark inside of her that lives inside of me too.

But that spark has landed us in trouble, and it's all my fucking fault.

"So, you're the one he chose," Jessica says to Kat as she looks her up and down like she's a piece of shit on her shoe. But the truth is, Jessica was always a jealous bitch, and it's so obvious that Kat is way above her and totally in a different league. The really creepy part about all of this is the fact that Jessica and Nate were never an item—not to my knowledge anyway. He would never have gone for her, and this is just the ridiculous play of a bunny boiler who thinks this is going to get her the life that she always wanted. Pah. Yeah. Good luck with that when Nate gets here and releases me to end your sorry existence, Jessica.

"Tell me, does it feel good to fuck what belongs to me?" Jessica says, continuing her perusal of Kat. She continues to witter on, and I will my big brother to get here and save us from the mess I have made of this mission. I guess that's why he's the brains and I've never been at the forefront of operations in the underworld, because I clearly don't think shit through enough before acting.

"Rock hard abs, thick thighs, and the best ass I've ever seen… I don't like when others play with my toys," she continues as I zone in and out, but that is where my patience for this crap ends.

"Jesus, Jessica, can you cut it with the details… that is my brother you're talking about," I snap, and the next thing I know, one of her fucking guard dogs—and by that, I mean gross, sweaty men—comes over and sticks tape over my mouth.

"Always had a motor mouth that one," Jessica says in reference to me.

*Bitch.* And with my mouth taped, she witters on some more before her next words have my heart trying to beat out of my chest...

"I think Mrs Knowles needs a taste of what it's like when you take something that isn't yours... Have your fun first before you finish her off," she instructs her men, and then they are quickly tying rope around Kat's legs. *No, no, no, they can't take her.*

"And if you're thinking about those biker men coming to rescue you, then don't. They're all dead," Jessica says, and I swear the fucking pain in my heart is like a knife ripping me apart, but I don't have time to process anything more when Jessica says, "Ruin her," as they remove the cuffs and get ready to carry Kat out of here.

I wildly thrash my arms and legs around, praying to a God that I don't believe in to throw me a fucking bone or some shit to get out of this and help Kat, but instead of a bone, I see the fucking devil has answered my silent plea.

Because there, stood in the doorway, looking as evil as ever is my brother, Lucas. The brother that killed our parents. The one that always put his needs before anyone else's. The man who thrives on pain, suffering and power. *Fuck.*

"Hi, sis," Lucas says, a smirk crossing his mouth, and my panic from moments ago multiplies ten-fold. "It's been a long time." *Yeah, it sure has, it's just a shame it's not been even longer.*

At Lucas' request, the tape is removed from my mouth by one of the guard dogs, and I struggle to form words.

"You didn't really think I'd just disappeared never to be seen again, did you?" he says. *Well, I lived in hope, but fate obviously had other shit in store, clearly.* Lucas turns his attention to Kat and then starts to give her a quick intro to who the hell he is. He admits to killing our parents and then makes his hatred and jealousy of Nate known—something I always knew. He always wanted everything Nate had, and I mean everything. Women, school friends, grades, even the fucking lunchbox that our mum used to pack his sandwiches in.

"Turns out, no one really liked me much, and they all chose Nate over me. So, I bided my time, went underground, kept silent, and now, here I am, ready and waiting for him to come here to rescue you both… and he won't even see the trap as he comes in here. He won't be thinking clearly, and it will pave the way for me to capture him and torture him before he meets his maker," he says to Kat as I try to pull myself out of the shock my body currently seems to be in.

"Just think how he will cope without his wife and his sister. Doesn't bare thinking about really, does it?" he taunts, and the thought shatters my heart. It would kill Nate to be without us both, I know it would, and I know that he would give up and let Lucas do whatever he wanted to him. Tears sting the backs of my eyes and I furiously blink them back as they start to distort my vision.

"It'll make him careless to know that I have you both," he says with a grin.

"Lucas, please don't do this," I plead, trying to reach some part of my brother that may still be somewhat human.

"Why not? Because we can all be one big happy family?" He laughs at me. "I don't fucking think so. Now, take her away and make sure we hear her screams," he says to the two guys, and then he's stepping aside and the guard dogs are taking Kat from the room. I scream and thrash about, but I'm rendered useless, and I know that I won't be able to live with myself after this. I know that if they hurt Kat and Nate doesn't get to her in time then I will never forgive myself.

"Now all we have to do is wait for the big bad crime lord to show up, and then the real fun starts," Lucas says as he walks into the room and stands beside Jessica. She looks at him with a mixture of fear and lust. Ugh. She really has no morals.

"Please, Lucas, I'm begging you to let Kat go. Please," I try to reason with him, but I already know it's pointless.

"I have absolutely no interest in rescuing some tart of Nate's," he replies, looking bored as fuck. "She's just bait, and you were an added bonus."

"And you wonder why everyone hated you," I grit out, anger running through my body at this whole situation.

"Oof," he says sarcastically, pretending I've wounded him by placing his hand on his heart.

"Why didn't you just stay away, huh?" I continue. "You're a fucking parasite—"

"And you're a fucking bitch," he shouts at me, cutting me off. Good, I appear to have pissed him off. If I can keep him talking, then it may distract him so Nate can come on in here and kill the bastard. "You always did suck up to fucking Nate. Everyone did. He was the best, he was the worthy one, meanwhile I'd just be stood there wondering what the fuck I ever did wrong."

"Really? You actually asked yourself that question after all the years of taunting and hurting me and Nate?" I ask incredulously. "All of the times you laughed at us when we fell over, or what about when you would push us and act like it was an accident—and then there was the time that I busted my lip because I came off of my bike after you rammed the front wheel of yours into the back of mine."

"That was just child's play," he retorts. Figures. He never did know how to show remorse.

"You can call it what you want, Lucas, but I call it bullying."

He stares long and hard at me, but I don't back down. If he's going to kill me, then I want to look the fucker right in the eyes as he does.

"Baby sis, I'm sorry it had to end like this… well, actually, I'm not really, and I will take great pleasure in finally bringing Nate to his fucking knees. It's his turn to beg for mercy, beg for life, but I'll never give him that.

"I'll torture him until he struggles to breathe, and then I'll rip out his fucking heart and lodge a bullet in his brain at the same time, because I couldn't decide which ending was better, so I'll just go with both." He's clearly done with the slight recap on our childhood, and I guess this is where it all ends. There is no reasoning with him, and my time is up.

"Lucas, you promised me that I could have my fun before you ended him," Jessica says.

"And you can. You can jump around on his dick as much as you like until I decide that it is enough," Lucas says, and I can hear the warning in his tone.

"You two are fucking sick," I tell them, disgust clear in my voice.

"You always knew this about me, sis, and I never pretended to be anything else," Lucas replies. "And you know what else, dear sister of mine?"

There is a pause as he takes a step towards me.

"I'm going to make sure that I retell the story to him over and over again about how his pretty little wife was raped repeatedly as she begged for her life."

His words make me shudder. Kat is the sister I never had, and I hope to God that by some miracle she gets out of here safely.

And it looks like my prayer has just been answered as Lucas' features go slack and he drops like a sack of shit to the floor, to reveal Nate stood behind him with a gun in his hand. Oh thank fuck.

Nate turns the gun on Jessica and her mouth drops open as her eyes go wide. "Nate," she whispers as her hands come up in front of her. "Please... I didn't... Please don't..."

"Spare me the fucking pity party," Nate snarls as he walks into the room. "You fucked with the wrong brother," he says, and I see that he's getting ready to pull the trigger, and I shout, "No, Nate."

He pauses and looks at me questioningly.

"Let me do it," I tell him, because I want to do this. I want to take this burden from him and end it once and for all. I worry he will never get over killing a woman, it's not something he's done previously, and I don't want him to take this on when it's my fault anyway.

"Get the key, let me out of these cuffs, and then I'll kill her," I say, *determination running through me.* "It won't be my first time," I add on, shocking the shit out of him. *Yeah, I've killed and kept it secret, but I don't have time to answer the questions that I know will be rattling around his head right now. We can talk later, but now is the time for action.*

"Where's the key?" *he barks at Jessica, and she quickly goes to get it and then frees me from the chains.*

"Oh, I'm going to enjoy this," *I say as it takes me less than half a second to plough my fist straight into her face. She drops to the floor, and I walk over to Nate, taking the gun from him and pointing it at her.* "Bye bye, Jessica. Sweet dreams." *I pull the trigger, and it's lights out for her.*

*Silence fills the room for a beat before Nate turns to me and says,* "Where's Kat?"

The pain of that day is still very real. I will never forget the way my heart beat uncontrollably, or how it broke when Nate, Kat and I finally left the place where it all went to hell and drove past the dead bodies lining the driveway. Every single biker that came to help me died. And when I saw Jason, I don't know how I held myself together. His eyes were open, looking up to the sky, his mouth hanging open slightly, the life gone from him.

And that will forever be the last image of him ingrained in my memory.

It taints everything that came before that, and I know the image will never leave me.

I can't take back what happened, but if I could rewind the clock, I would.

Instead of staying and facing up to what had happened, I ran away. I came to this idyllic island with Kat and Nate, and I never looked back.

But the urge to return is there. It always has been. And working through my grief has made that urge so much stronger.

I couldn't face it before. I know that their deaths were my fault, but I couldn't accept it fully when my heart was breaking too.

But now I can.

I've had some therapy, and I've worked through as much as I can here, but in order to truly heal, I have to go back and face the demons that may await me.

All I have to do now is tell my big brother and hope that he doesn't block me from truly allowing my heart to heal.

## Chapter Two

### Zoey

"Auntie Zoey," I hear Gracie shout from the bottom of the stairs. "Dinner time." Even the sound of her voice melts my heart. She's the sweetest kid ever, and I love her to pieces.

"Coming," I shout back to her as I put my phone down on the bedside table and make my way downstairs. I had been making sure I was up to speed with anything happening back in the UK, namely where we used to live, and I've been doing it since we left. But recently, I've been searching more. It's that pull to go back, it's taking all of my head space.

I leave my room and make my way down the stairs, following the delicious scent of whatever Kat has been whipping up in the kitchen.

When I enter the dining space—which is just to the right of the open-plan kitchen—I see Nate and Gracie sat at the table, talking quietly amongst themselves, Gracie chuckling at something he's said. God, that chuckle makes me all gooey inside, and it pains me that I don't already have a family of my own. I mean, don't get me wrong, I love being with Nate, Kat and Gracie, but my mind always wanders back and asks, *"What if?"*

What if things had turned out differently?

What if Jason and I had still been together?

What if we had had our own kids by now?

Ugh. Shut up.

In all the years since we moved here, there's been no one else. I haven't even entertained the thought, and at thirty-six years old, my biological clock is ticking away and reminding me that I don't have all the time in the fucking world. But every time I even think about going on a date or hooking up with another guy, it makes me feel wrong. Like I shouldn't be doing it. Like I'm not meant to have that kind of happiness.

Maybe it's my punishment for what happened?

I walk to the kitchen table and sit down opposite Gracie as she looks at me with a smile. "And what are you two whispering about?" I ask her and Nate, because I can see the mischief in both of their eyes.

"Promise you won't tell Mummy?" Gracie says, and I move my finger to my heart and draw a cross.

"Cross my heart," I tell her.

"Can I tell her, Daddy?" she says to Nate, and he gives her a nod whilst smiling.

"We're going on a trip," she whispers.

"Ooo, that's exciting. And where might this trip be?" I ask her.

"To Africa, for Mummy's birthday," she says excitedly.

"Oh wow. She's going to love that," I say, knowing that going there and going on safari has been a life-long dream of Kat's.

"But shush," Gracie says as she covers her lips with her finger. "It's a secret."

I give her a wink as Kat comes over and places a large dish in the middle of the table.

"Oh yum, a roast dinner," I say as I see the meat already carved, along with roast potatoes, vegetables, stuffing, and of course, Yorkshire puddings. Kat brings over a pot of gravy before sitting down on the other side of Gracie and picking up her glass of… water?

"No wine?" I ask Kat with a frown. She always has a glass of wine with dinner, as do I. Only the one, unless we're having a couple more out in the garden, but that's not very often. Neither of us are massive drinkers, and Nate is just a one or two beers kind of guy.

"I just don't feel like wine tonight, I've been feeling a bit off," she says whilst looking shifty.

"Mmmhmm," I mumble, taking a sip of my own crisp pinot grigio—which she had already poured before I came in here. Honestly, she's a proper homemaker, and I love how she doesn't make me feel like I'm in the way or unwanted. Our bond has been special from the start, and we know each other inside out. Which is why, with her not drinking wine, I already know that she's pregnant—or that she thinks she might be—she doesn't have to tell me. And how I contain my excitement, I do not fucking know, but I can't say anything, not with Gracie here and totally unaware that she may be about to become a big sister. But once she's out of earshot, I'm going to be jumping for joy.

Seeing Nate become a dad is one of the best things I've ever witnessed, and he's really settled into family life. I'm so happy for him—and for Kat—but seeing it every day makes me want to completely heal, so that maybe I can have that kind of family life too.

"Are you okay, Mummy?" Gracie says, concern all over her little face.

"I'm fine, sweetie. Now, come on, let's eat before this gets cold," Kat says as she starts to dish Gracie's food onto her plate. I look at Nate, but he busies himself dishing up his food, avoiding my gaze… oh yeah, she's definitely pregnant.

We manage to get through dinner with light chatter—little Gracie doing most of the talking. She's got her first day at school tomorrow and she's so excited.

"Will you come too, Auntie Zoey?" she asks me with those big, beautiful green eyes.

"Of course I will," I tell her, and she squeals before asking to leave the table and running off into the playroom before she has to have a bath and get ready for bed.

"So, now that she's not here, are one of you going to confirm what I already know?" I say, unable to keep quiet any longer.

Nate looks to Kat, and her eyes flit to him as she bites her bottom lip, trying to stop the smile from spreading across her face as she says, "Yes, I'm pregnant, but—"

I cut her off as I let out an excited squeal and quickly make my way around the table to give her a hug. Kat laughs at my excitement, and then I move to my brother and give him a hug too.

"Okay, okay," he says, but he can't stop the shit eating grin from spreading across his face. "Calm down, we don't want to tell Gracie yet."

"You want to wait until the three-month mark?" I ask, and they both nod. I get it, but damn is it going to be hard to keep my mouth shut… although… this could be perfect timing…

"Obviously I am over the moon for you guys, but I need to talk to you…" I sit back down in my seat as they both look at me, their smiles fading slowly.

"What's wrong?" Kat asks as she scoots forward on her chair, her eyebrows drawn together slightly.

"Nothing's wrong… I just… I…" Why is this so hard to say?

"Zoey?" Nate says, and I see the concern on his face.

*Fuck's sake, Zoey, just spit it out already.*

"I want to go home," I blurt out, and they both frown.

"You are home," Kat says with a chuckle, but Nate stays quiet, assessing me. He already knows where I want to go. Damn me for being so easy to read sometimes.

"She means back to the UK," Nate says, and Kat's mouth drops open.

"But why?" she asks. "Don't you like living here?"

"Of course I do. I love being here with you guys and Gracie, but I feel this pull to go back, to finally try and work through the last bit of feeling guilty…" I let my voice trail off as images of Jason flit through my mind. Of how he made me feel, of how we once were.

"Oh, Zoey," Kat says as she reaches her hand across the table and covers mine, squeezing gently. "I thought you had moved past all of that?"

"I have, for the most part. But this is just something I have to do. To heal completely." I don't expect them to totally get it. Why would they? They've worked through every obstacle they have come across and have the perfect family life. They have no guilt left, but I do, and I need to deal with it once and for all.

"I'll make arrangements, just tell me when you want to

leave," Nate says as he takes a sip of his beer, his eyes homed in on me.

The shock on my face must be clear, because I never expected him to accept this so easily. "You mean, you're not going to try and talk me out of it?"

"Look, Zoey," he says as he places his beer back down and sighs. "If you really do feel like this is what you need to do, then I'm not going to stop you. Lord knows you'll never give up on this idea and you'll chew my ear off until it happens, and I have no desire to put my ear canals through that, thank you very much."

"Hey," I say as I playfully reach across and punch him on the arm. Kat chuckles, and I smile.

"But on a serious note," Nate continues. "I will make all of the arrangements, so I know that you're safe. And I'll only do it on the condition that you come back."

"Always with the conditions," I say with an eye roll.

"I mean it, Zoey. I understand that you need to do this for you, but I don't want you staying there. We may have been gone for years, but ultimately, my name still means something over there, and that means that yours does too." I can see the worry on his face, but I have no intentions of not returning to this idyllic island. I'll be back, just as soon as I figure out what is going to finally shut off that guilt switch once and for all.

"I'll come back, brother. I promise."

## Chapter Three

### Zoey

"Are you sure you packed everything you need?" Kat says as we walk into the airport, her, Nate and Gracie following behind me.

"I'm sure, Kat. Stop stressing," I say with a chuckle, but the chuckle is forced. My emotions are all over the fucking place as the day has come for me to return to the UK. The place where my life fell apart five years ago. I'm trying to act calm because I don't want my family to worry about me anymore than they already are. I see it in Nate's eyes, and I hear it in Kat's voice. A part of me wishes they were coming too, but I know that Nate would never do that and possibly put Gracie in harm's way. And I get it. I wouldn't either if the roles were reversed. But at the same time, I know it's killing both of them not to be coming with me.

I move through the airport until I get to the correct check-in desk, where I am greeted by a bubbly woman who some may think had snorted too many lines of coke already today. Seriously, she's that cheerful.

After I've checked in, she wishes me "bon voyage," and I move to the side so the person behind me can be greeted by her over enthusiastic nature. I turn to my family to see Nate has his jaw clenched, Kat is blinking furiously to hold back tears, and Gracie is busy looking out of the floor-to-ceiling windows behind me at the planes as they take off intermittently.

"Well, this is me," I say with a shrug, because they can't come through to the waiting lounge without a ticket.

"I'm going to miss you," Kat says before she launches herself at me and wraps her arms around my shoulders, pulling me in for the mother of all hugs.

"Those hormones are already working overtime, huh?" I say, and I hear her sniffle. She had her doctor's appointment two days ago, and it was confirmed that she is indeed pregnant. Fourteen weeks pregnant, to be exact.

"You know I'm going to be a bloody mess whilst you're gone, right?" she says dramatically as she pulls back to look at me.

"You'll be fine," I reassure her. "And if he pisses you off too much, I'm at the end of the phone," I say as I nod my head in Nate's direction.

"I heard that," he says, and both Kat and I laugh.

"You better be back before this baby comes," Kat says, and I swallow down the lump that has suddenly formed in my throat.

"I will be. I wouldn't miss it for the world," I tell her truthfully. I may have no return date planned at present, but there is no way that I would miss my niece or nephew being brought into this world. It would break my heart to not be here for it.

Kat steps back, wiping her eyes as I bend down to give Gracie a hug.

"Now, missy, you make sure you keep your dad in check while I'm gone," I tell her, and she salutes at me.

"I will, Auntie Zoey."

"And I'll make sure to facetime as much as I can," I say, and I'm pretty sure I'm going to be on the phone for most of my time away.

"I love you," she says before dropping a kiss on my cheek. Oh fuck, my heart.

"Love you too, Gracie." I clench my teeth to stop the emotions from overflowing. I can cry when they've gone. Just my goodbye with Nate to get through first.

I stand up and look at my brother. He's really stepped up since he met Kat. At one time, we may have had some distance between us, but not anymore. Our bond is solid, unbreakable, and he's more than made up for the times he may have been absent from my life.

"Gonna miss you, big bro," I say as I lightly punch him on the arm. I may be in my mid-thirties—and him in his early forties—but we still act as we always have, ribbing each other when we feel the need and acting like we did way back when.

He pulls me in for a hug and I squeeze my eyes shut. Just a few more minutes and then the tears can fall.

"You get any problems, you know I'm just a phone call and a plane ride away," he tells me, and I know without a shadow of a doubt that if I truly needed him, then he would be there.

"I know," I whisper as I give him one final squeeze and move back. "I'll be back before you know it," I tell them as I grab the handle on my suitcase and get ready to go through the doors to the departure lounge.

"Call us when you get there," Kat says, silent tears running down her cheeks as Nate puts his arm around her and pulls her to him, and I nod at her.

My family.

Picture perfect.

An image that I mentally take to give me comfort whilst I'm away.

"Bye, guys," I say, because I can't say anything more. My throat is clogged with unshed tears as I turn my back on them and make my way through the departure door, hearing it close quietly behind me.

*"Jason, I need your help,"* I tell him through the phone.

*"What's up?"* he says, and I take a deep breath.

*"I'm at my house... Bring a clean-up crew with you."*

*"What have you done, Zoey?"* he asks, and I grit my teeth together to stop from letting my emotions unleash.

*"You'll see. Just hurry. Please."* I end the call and place the phone down on the kitchen table as I take deep breaths to try and calm myself down.

*Twenty minutes ago, I was leaving the restaurant where I had a date.*

*Fifteen minutes ago, I knew I was being followed.*

*Ten minutes ago, I fought off my attacker as they tried to drag me down a dark alley so they could do fuck knows what with me.*

*Five minutes ago, I killed my date—my attacker.*

*And now, here I am, stood in my kitchen with my attacker laying outside on the cold concrete, dead. Luckily, I have high fucking walls around my property, but it was still a struggle to drag his sorry ass onto the driveway before anyone could see what I had done. And luckily, I don't have a shitload of neighbours.*

*I toy with the idea of phoning Nate. He'd help me in a heartbeat, but he's been distant recently, and I know he's going through his own shit—not to mention that he recently got married.*

*No.*

*I need to try and sort this out myself—or with the help of the biker crew that I just phoned. Jason and I have been friends for a while now. We met at the bar I own—Purity. Our friendship grew from sarcasm, wit and, of course, flirting. Jason is so fucking easy on the eye that my pussy tingles just from the sight of him. Hot doesn't even cover it, and don't get me started on his brother, Jaxon—or rather, Jax, as he likes to be addressed. Together, any other men pale in comparison. But Jason is easier to get along with than Jax. Jason is the light, whereas Jax is the dark—like a cold fish. You never know where you fucking stand with Jax, and I don't have the patience to deal with that, even if he is ridiculously handsome.*

*I hear the roar of a bike outside, and I make my way to the front door on shaky legs. Fuck, I need to get it together. I'm the sister of a goddamn crime lord for fuck's sake, this shit should come easy. Nate deals with killing people so often that I am sure he wouldn't have batted an eyelid at what I have done, but I have never been interested in that side of things. I've fiercely held onto my compassion and humanity all of these years, only for it to be taken in one swift move by a dickhead that didn't understand the word 'no.'*

*I open the front door and see Jason on the other side of the gates, waiting to be let in. I tap a button by the front door and the gates begin to open. As soon as there is enough room for him to fit through, he does, coming to a stop in front of me as I stand on the porch, my arms wrapped around myself, my eyes refusing to look to the right where the dead guy lies underneath some bushes.*

*Jason takes his helmet off and I see the concern in his eyes as they lock with mine.*

*"Are you okay?" he asks as he kicks out the bike stand and then gets*

*off and moves towards me. He places his hands on either side of my face, cupping my cheeks and tilting my head slightly.*

*My lip trembles, but I refuse to cry tears. Aaron—my date—deserved what he got. He doesn't deserve my remorse or guilt.*

*I look into Jason's light brown eyes, and I feel the change from flirty banter to something more. Him being here means more. But I don't have time to think about it as I hear more bikes coming down the road.*

*"I'm fine, but he isn't," I say as I move my hand and hold my arm out, pointing in the direction of Aaron's body. Jason's eyes move from me to where I'm pointing, before they come back to meet mine again.*

*"What did he do?" he asks.*

*"He tried to force me down an alleyway, and I'm pretty sure I don't have to tell you anything else," I say as his hands still cradle my face.*

*Three bikes roar through the gates and come to a stop just behind Jason's bike.*

*"We'll sort it," Jason says, placing a kiss on my forehead before dropping his hands from my face and turning to go and speak to his guys. As they take their helmets off, I see Cole, Kev, and of course, Jax. His dark brown eyes lock with mine over Jason's shoulder, but there is no emotion there. He's so fucking closed off it's ridiculous. But then, I don't know his story, and he sure as shit doesn't know mine, so really, there should be no judging one another at this point.*

*I've tried talking to him, but the conversation never goes very deep, and he tends to only answer with the bare minimum when asked a question. The untouchable brother. And maybe that's a good thing, because when he does talk, it gives me all the fucking flutters. I mean, seriously, the dude has a voice that would melt your damn knickers off.*

*I almost laugh to myself.*

*Here I am, lusting after Jason and Jax, and not ten fucking feet from me is a guy I've killed. Couldn't make this shit up.*

*"Let's go," I hear Jason say as he moves over to the body, Cole and*

Kev following him. My eyes move back to Jax, who is still sat on his bike, his attention still on me.

I raise my chin a little, so he knows that I don't feel intimidated by him. He should know that anyway though. I see a small smirk grace his lips as he gets off of his bike and comes over, stopping just in front of me. If I were to step forward, I'd be touching him.

"You need us to clean up your mess, pretty girl?" Jax says, and his words thrill me and piss me off at the same time.

"First off, I'm not a girl. And second, I called Jason to help, not you."

"Maybe, but you know that where he is, I am," Jax tells me, and it's true. Neither of them are ever far from the other one.

"If you're here to help, then great, but if you're just here to give me a hard time, then save yourself the bother. It's been a shitter of a night and I don't wish for it to get any worse," I say, because I don't need the grief. All I need is for this to be over and to be in the shower, washing away any remnants of this evening.

"Did he hurt you?" he asks.

"I'm fine," I grit out, because he doesn't really give a shit.

"I asked you a question, Zoey."

"So what? Just because you're Jaxon Jones and leader of the club, that means I have to give you answers?" I retort.

"Something like that," he says, and I take a step towards him, pushing my chest against his, tilting my head up, our faces inches apart.

"I don't have to answer to you, Jax, and I never will."

"Don't fuck with me, Zoey."

"Or what?" I say with an eyebrow raised.

"Just because my brother wants a piece of your pussy doesn't mean I'm going to let you walk all over me," he grits out before turning away and walking over to where the other guys are doing fuck knows what to the body. They're all crowded around and hunched over, so I can't see anyway, and I really don't care at this moment in time.

That might just be one of the longest conversations Jax and I have *ever had, and all it showed me is that his walls are so fucking high that even spiderman couldn't scale them.*

*Easy on the eye he may be, but that doesn't make up for the fact that he is an asshole.*

*I see Jason turn around to look at me with a wink and a smile, and my face transforms in an instant. He's so different, and with Jax's revelation that Jason does actually want to be acquainted with my pussy, it seems that my life may just become a little more eventful than it was before tonight.*

I wake with a start, feeling hot and bothered.

It takes me a second to get my bearings and remember that I'm on a fucking plane. Going back to England. To face my demons.

Should I really be doing this?

Should I be stirring up old shit that may be best left in the past?

"We will be preparing to land in fifteen minutes." The announcement comes over the speakers.

Fifteen minutes and I'll be on home soil.

Fifteen minutes until I go back to face my nightmares.

Fifteen minutes… fuck.

## Chapter Four

### Zoey

I arrive back at my old house. I never sold it, never thought about it once I moved away. It wasn't important. It was just a building that held little meaning to me. The only reason I knew I still had it is because Nate told me that he was making sure it was being maintained all of these years, and of course, Nate being Nate, he refused to do anything with it until I mentioned it to him. Same goes for Purity—my club. It's still mine. Still running. Still going on without me.

Purity was once my happy place. My haven. But now, I don't know where my happy place is.

"Thanks," I say to Ronan, the guy who picked me up from the airport and drove me back here—and the guy that took over the running of things when Nate decided to leave.

"No problem," he says as he takes my bags out of the car.

"How's things been since we've been gone?" I ask him, because I feel like I need to know that they are running things right. I know it's none of my business, but I've never been great at keeping my nose out where it doesn't concern me.

"It was strange at first, you know, without Nate's guidance, but he's been there when I've needed to ask him anything," he tells me as he places the last bag on the floor and shuts the car. I always liked Ronan. He may now be running the crime world, but he's always had a quality about him that made me warm to him instantly. "Does he miss it?"

"I don't think so," I answer truthfully. "Once he met Kat, I think he knew that there was more to life."

He nods his head, his blonde locks bouncing slightly around his shoulders.

"I get it. I saw it. She's a good one," he says, and I couldn't agree more. She made my brother see things differently. "It's good to have you back though, Zozo," he says before stepping towards me and giving me a hug. Zozo. His nickname for me. It makes me smile.

He lets me go and steps back, and suddenly, a wave of emotion hits me and I have to swallow past the lump that has formed in my throat.

"Anyone would think that you missed me," I say, trying to keep it light and inject a little humour so I don't have a full-on emotional meltdown in front of him.

"Like a hole in the head," he says with a smile, and I laugh. It's good to laugh. I need to remember that as I try to heal the last part of me that remains scarred. "You need anything, you call me."

"Sure," I say as I pick up one of my bags and hook it over my shoulder.

"I mean it, Zoey. Anything, anytime."

"Thanks, Ronan." I quickly turn to the front door, but

then I realise that I don't have a set of keys to this place anymore.

"Here," I hear Ronan say from behind me, and then I see his arm appearing in front of me, dangling my keys in front of my face. They still have the keyring attached that Jason gave me. A silver heart with a motorcycle in the middle of it. He gave it to me because he said he had two loves in this life—bikes and me. I take a deep breath and furiously blink back the tears that want to escape. Not yet. Not in front of Ronan.

I quickly move my hand and take the keys, moving forward to unlock the door. I push it open and am immediately hit by a citrus scent.

"I've been making sure the place remains clean. Couldn't have you coming back to it smelling all musty and shit," Ronan says, and I have to be thankful that his loyalty to my family runs deep.

"Thank you," I say as I take a step inside and look around. Nothing has changed. Same décor. Same pictures on the walls. Same house. Different woman. I'm different to who I was when I left here five years ago.

"Want me to take these bags upstairs?" Ronan says.

"No, it's okay, but thank you," I say, still with my back to him. I just need him to go. I need a moment.

"I'll check in with you in a day or two," he says, and then I hear him leave, the door closing behind him.

"Well, Zoey, you're here, and now you have to face all the shit that you've been avoiding for years," I say out loud to myself, suddenly realising how alone I feel.

After unpacking my clothes and the items I brought back with me, I crashed in my old bedroom, clearly more exhausted than I realised. The emotions are still raging through me this morning as I sip my cup of coffee and sit at my kitchen table, but I intend to power through. I'm not going to hide out here, not when I came to get the peace I long for.

I'm a fucking Knowles, and I need to start remembering how to act like one.

I finish my coffee, and with determination, I go back to my bedroom and get changed out of my pyjamas. I put on my skinny denim jeans, a white sleeveless shirt, a wrap-around white jacket, and my black boots. I apply makeup and run my fingers through my long black hair, opting to leave it with a slight wave running through the strands. After appraising myself in the mirror one last time, I make my way back downstairs and grab my car keys hanging on the hook by the front door. I presume my car is still here, and when I unlock the door to the garage and step inside, I can see that it is, and it looks like it's been just as well looked after as the house has been.

I don't ever feel weird that everything has been looked after. I mean, most may find it strange, but not when you have Nate as a brother. Fucker takes care of everything.

I slip inside my range rover and start it up. As the music comes on, I see that even my playlist hasn't been fucked with. I smile and click the button on my keys to open the garage door, sliding my sunglasses on as the sun starts to peek underneath the door as it opens.

I relax back into the seat and drive out slowly when the door has finished opening, making my way along the drive and to the gate. I don't even need to flick a button for the gate to open as I pull up to it, because there is some type of recognition thing that automatically recognises my car and means I don't have to faff around with a button or anything. Honestly, this is another level type shit, but Nate only ever had the very best installed in my house—and his.

I pull out onto the main road and drive down the quiet street. With very few houses dotted along the sides, it's hardly surprising that I see no one around until I venture closer to the town. I drive past the shops that I used to frequent on a daily basis, nostalgia hitting me at every turn. How Nate and I as kids used to grab sweets from the corner shop, flanked by security and an ever-present nanny. How we used to go to the park after and play on the swings. How our brother Lucas used to always be stood off to the side, never bothering to join in unless there was an element of danger to our play.

My memories with Lucas are not my favourite, but the ones with Nate are. And then shit got all screwed as we got older and Lucas got more jealous of Nate, until the time came when he killed our parents because he thought that would automatically hand him the crown to rule.

I keep going past the park until I am pulling through the gates of the church and driving slowly along the track that will take me around the back to the cemetery.

I pull to a stop and see that my car is the only one here. I guess that a Tuesday morning isn't the most popular time to be visiting the dead.

I take a deep breath and get out of my car, locking it behind me as I make my way to the graves that are to my left. My feet wander to the first grave that I came here to visit, the one where both of my parents have been laid to rest. Fresh flowers line the headstone, the grave itself immaculately free of weeds.

"Hi, Mum and Dad," I say as I crouch down by the gravestone and run my fingers over the engraved lettering. '*Feared by most, loved by many*'. It's true. People may have feared my family, but they were loved by those that mattered. I smile as I am reminded of my dad, and of how he was truly so different to the man that used to tuck me in at night and read me a bedtime story. He did what he had to do, but at home, he was just 'Dad.'

And my mother, she was a radiant beauty who did anything her family needed her to do. She cherished and loved us unconditionally. She taught us compassion but also reminded us that we needed to stay smart and learn how to wheedle out the people that would want to take us down. You couldn't always tell, and the saga with Jessica is proof of that, but for the most part, Nate and I did okay.

"I miss you both so much," I whisper. "I wish you could see Nate now, as a dad, living his best life as a husband and father. You would have both loved Gracie so much. She's the sweetest, and Kat too. You would laugh at how she challenges Nate but also loves him with everything she has. She's a good one, and he's the man I always knew he would be.

"But I'm lost. I've been lost for a while now. My life isn't as I thought it would be," I say as a tear rolls down my cheek. "I can't seem to let go of the past. I can't stop the thoughts from coming back to haunt me. I need to heal, I need to grieve properly, and I'm here to do that and make you both proud of me too…" My voice breaks as I say the last words.

All I ever wanted to do was make them proud and live my best life. I haven't been doing that, but I want to be.

"I don't know how long I'll be here for, but I'll come again before I leave. I'm sorry it's been five years since I last visited, but I see Nate has made sure that your grave is all tidy with fresh flowers. He always did think of everything," I say with a chuckle. Nate is very much like how my dad was—always in control, always getting the job done. It's why he was made the crime lord over Lucas. Lucas would have brought nothing but terror to everyone that so much as looked at him wrong.

"I love you both," I say as I place a kiss on my fingertips and then press them to the stone before standing and taking a look around me. I know who I'm looking for next, but I also have no idea if they had a cremation or a burial. I imagine a burial, but you never know, and I never made contact to ask, so I'll go in search myself.

I walk along each of the pathways slowly, reading name after name on the head stones. I'm not in a rush, and if this takes me all day, then so be it.

It's only when I walk further along the paths and see a group of people gathered around and over to my far left that I freeze, a shiver running through me.

Why are they all here?

What are they doing?

And with those question comes the realisation of what the day is. August twenty-fourth. The five-year anniversary of Jason's death. How could I have let the date slip my mind? And how could I have not realised that I'd be coming back here exactly five years to the day that my whole life changed? Fuck.

They can't see me here—they'll gut me like a fucking fish. And just like that, I turn and hightail it out of here. I know I said I was a Knowles and I needed to start acting like one, but I'll try again tomorrow. There's no way I am walking into the fucking firing line today, not with all of them there, and not with Jax Jones in the middle of them, probably baying for my blood.

# Chapter Five

## Jax

She thinks I don't see her, but I do.

I already knew she was back in town. I don't have informants for nothing, so it comes as no surprise that she runs away like the fucking coward she is when she sees us all stood around Jason's grave.

Did she not think we would be here?

Did she think that we just forgot about it like she fucking did?

I've been waiting five years to see her again. I even sent guys to try and find her, but they could never find a trace. Until now. And she is going to wish that she had never come back.

# Chapter Six

## Zoey

"Hey, Gracie," I say as her face appears on the phone.

"Auntie Zoey," she says whilst clapping her hands. "Are you coming back?"

"Not just yet, sweetie," I tell her.

"Ohhh," she says as she pouts and crosses her arms over her chest, making me chuckle. "Daddy, Auntie Zoey isn't coming back," she shouts before she runs off and leaves me staring at the kitchen wall. Seconds later, my big brother comes on the screen, looking all serious and shit.

"You're not coming back?" he questions straight away.

I roll my eyes before answering. "Not yet, no. Jeez, it's only been two days, Nate, and Gracie left out the 'not yet' part of my answer."

"Oh," he says, his shoulders instantly relaxing. "So, has there been any trouble?"

"Again, two days," I repeat. "You're not the crime lord now, brother, so chill out a little bit."

"I'll always be the crime lord, but all right, I get your point, I'll chill out."

I laugh at him because Nate doesn't know how to chill out when it comes to me, Kat or Gracie, but I'll humour him for the time being.

"Is Ronan keeping an eye on things?" he asks, being so unsubtle it's ridiculous.

"You know damn well that Ronan keeps a tab on everything, including me, but I don't need him to have someone follow me twenty-four seven, thank you very much." I forgot what this part of my life was like. The security that always stays close, the heavies ready to take someone out at the slightest hint of trouble. I didn't have anyone follow me to the grave on my first day back, but since then, I've noticed a car parked across the road, and I know that Ronan has one of his guys out there. It's a safety precaution, I get it, but I can still look out for myself—as long as I don't run into the motorbike crew all at once. One or two I could handle, but all of them together, not so much. I guess I'll have to get creative again to give the security guys the slip sometimes, because I don't want my whole trip to be under surveillance. It's annoying and totally goes against the freedom I came here to find.

"I just want you to be safe," he says, as if he is telling me something I don't already know.

"I know." I smile and then decide to change the subject. "So, tell me what you guys have been up to and how my future niece or nephew is doing."

We talk for a bit longer and he fills me in on what I've missed during the last few days. Kat isn't there for me to speak to, she's at some school function thing because she's joined the parent committee. Good luck to the other parents because Kat is a force to be reckoned with.

The call ends and I say a last goodbye to Gracie before promising to call her again tomorrow—and every day after that. I'm also reminded by Nate that Ronan has a driver on hand for me at all times, and I am to call them if I go anywhere. I reassured him that I would—most of the time—even if it does bug me to do so. And with that thought in mind, I actually do call Ronan and request to be taken to my club this evening. It's time for me to visit a place that once fuelled my soul.

---

Walking back into Purity, I feel like I've been transported back in time. It hasn't changed at all, and I love it. It's something from my past that—most of the time—brought me joy from seeing what I had accomplished. Of course there was one time that Kat was attacked here by some crazy guy who worked for Lucas and Jessica, but usually, trouble was avoided—probably because I always had the best security here and anyone who knew Nate knew not to fuck around.

I walk along the balcony that sits just above the dance floor and smile when I see that Kayla is behind the bar. She's been here since I opened the club, and she knows the place inside out. I always trusted her to take care of things if I wasn't here, and it looks like she still is.

Her long blonde hair covers her face, before her head whips up and turns in my direction. I smile and walk over to the bar as she smirks.

"Zoey Knowles, long fucking time no speak, girl," she says

in greeting, quickly pouring a drink and passing it my way without even being asked.

I perch on a bar stool and take the drink from her. "Missed me?"

"Like a hole in the head," she says, smiling, and I laugh. We never did settle for the usual 'hi, how are you?' or 'good to see you.'

"So, what brings you back? Where the hell did you go? And is this a permanent thing?" she asks, ready to delve into why I'm here.

"Can a girl not come back and check on her business without getting a grilling?"

"Nope, not if you're Zoey Knowles you can't."

I sigh, not ready to have this conversation yet. It's been a long time since I confided in anyone other than Kat, and I'm not sure I'm ready to throw all my shit in Kayla's direction. I mean, I could, but I don't feel comfortable doing that. We may have gotten along when I was here before, but it's been five years since I saw her, and to be honest, I'm not totally comfortable with anyone knowing how I'm feeling right now.

"I see you're still pushy," I mutter as I take a sip of my drink. Vodka and cranberry juice. She remembered my drink of choice.

"And I see you're still good at diverting," she responds.

"Touché," I say as I place my glass back down.

"I get it, it's been a long time since we last spoke, but just know that I've always got your back. I wouldn't still be here if I didn't," she replies before she winks at me and turns away, walking to another spot at the bar as new customers start to walk in.

I never fully trusted many females when I lived here, always aware that I had to keep certain things guarded because of who we were and because of what my brother did, so I find it hard to open up. It was easy with Kat, seeing as she became my brother's wife. She automatically got my trust with just that one thing alone, but anyone else had to earn it, and very few even tried. But I guess now that my brother is no longer here, things should be a little easier… maybe. Maybe I can trust Kayla beyond a work capacity, but it's going to take more than one vodka and cranberry drink to make that decision.

I swivel on my stool and look around. People are dancing, drinking, and generally having a good time. It doesn't matter that it's not quite the weekend yet because there are always people ready to party, no matter what night of the week it is.

I finish my drink and decide to go to what used to be my office. As I make my way out of the main room and through the foyer, I see that Ronan is stood by the front doors, talking to a couple of the security guys. He nods in my direction as I walk past, and I smile. I haven't seen him since the day he picked me up from the airport, but we've exchanged a few messages and I've called him when I've needed to go anywhere—as instructed by Nate. He always was one of my favourites, and even though I've been gone for years, he hasn't made it weird, and it seems like we spoke just yesterday. It's nice, comforting, familiar. There was never anything between us other than friendship, and it's like he's a security blanket.

I walk past the VIP section where there is comfortable seating, a private courtyard, and a stage where the elite can watch exclusive performances ranging from singers to dance acts, and of course, this is where you will find the men who enjoy watching women on stage, dancing and swinging around a pole. It's cliché, I know, but it's all very tasteful, and no girl is here unless they want to be. They're paid extremely well, and they are not to be touched. Some may call it seedy, but I think they're wrong. It's sensual, mesmerizing, and only exclusive guests get to go in there and sip their scotch whilst they enjoy the entertainment.

At the end of the hallway, it opens up to give more space, with three doors spanning the back wall. One is for my office, one is for the staff room, and the third is for a dance studio where routines are practiced with the in-house choreographer before being perfected on the VIP stage. My office is the middle door and I key in the code that Ronan gave me earlier to unlock it. The codes are changed often for security purposes. As I hear the door click open, I push down the handle and am intrigued to see if anything has changed in here, but before I get the chance to even switch the light on, I'm shoved inside, the door quickly being slammed closed as I'm pinned against the wall, my cheek being pushed to the cold surface and a body encasing mine as my arms are held down at my sides by whoever the fuck is behind me. My eyes go wide as I try desperately to make out anything, but the room is pitch black. Fuck.

My heart starts to race, and fear runs through me, but I need to remember that I have lived in a world where danger lurks around every corner. I need to remember where I come from and who I am. I take deep, measured breaths as I try to exude some calm over my body and mind.

*I am Zoey Knowles. Sister of Nate, a once notorious crime lord in these parts. I've got this. I can deal with this—whatever the fuck 'this' is going to be.*

I repeat the words on a loop in my mind for what seems like forever as the person behind me just holds me in place. I don't squirm, I don't make a sound, and all that can be heard is the combined breaths of me and the predator behind me.

Because they can be nothing else, pinning me against the fucking wall and wanting to make me feel helpless.

I feel their breath on my cheek, their lips whispering over the shell of my ear before they say, "It's been a long time, pretty girl."

And my heart stops for a beat.

My senses heighten, taking in the scent that he wears, the sound of his gravelly voice, and the way his body moulds against mine.

I feel the tickle of his stubble on my ear as he speaks again. "Did you think I would forget?"

His voice, his words, they elicit guilt and excitement all at the same time. They render me speechless as I struggle to form a sentence—or even one fucking word.

And as much as I don't want them to, they make something stir inside of me that has been dormant for a long time. Something that died along with Jason… only to be reawakened by a man who keeps himself guarded and holds on to a grudge like no other.

A man who may very well have been baying for my blood since I left.

A man who could destroy me.

Jason's brother.

Closed off and cold-hearted.

Jax Jones.

## Chapter Seven

### Jax

I've waited a long fucking time to get my hands on Zoey Knowles.

I've been to hell and back trying to find her, only to run into a dead end each and every time.

I've wrestled with the anger that festers inside of me over my brother's death.

And now, here she is. Pinned to a wall in front of me and at my mercy.

Finally.

My body cages hers against the wall, my leg in-between hers, parting them slightly so she can't get a proper footing to try and shake me off her. Not that she would be able to, but I'm not taking any chances when it comes to her—the woman that is responsible for my brother being six feet under.

And seeing as she's been gone for what feels like forever, she has no idea of the power I hold in this world. She has no idea who the fuck I am, and I'm about to start my crusade in bringing her to her knees until she begs for mercy, only for her to meet the same end as my brother. Death. It's what she deserves.

"Did you think I would forget?" I growl in her ear, and I feel her body tense more, her muscles locked tight.

Seconds turn into minutes as I breathe her in and hope that she feels nothing but fear as I cage her in, milking this moment for all it's worth.

There was a time that I accepted her, because my brother found her pussy magical, but there's no acceptance now. I will not accept that she gets to walk around and live her life. She doesn't get to have her happy ending. Not on my watch.

Some may say I need to let this shit go and allow myself to grieve—something that actually *has* been said in the past—but I refuse to acknowledge those words. There is only vengeance and punishment on my mind, and being who I am today, I would never let anyone get away with hurting my family. People who come for me suffer, greatly, and Zoey Knowles will be no different.

The room is pitch black and all I can hear is Zoey trying to regulate her breathing. In slowly through the nose and out through the mouth. I just listen, allowing the anger to flow through me freely. My grip on her arms tightens, and I don't miss the hiss of pain that leaves her.

"Jax..." The first word she's spoken, her voice quiet and pained.

I could take her. Right now, I could take her. That was always my plan. To take her and make her suffer. I've become a ruthless bastard and I make no apology for that. And I certainly won't ever be swayed by a hot piece of ass. Because Zoey is hot, there is no mistaking that fact with her long black hair, her curves and her sea-green eyes that used to sparkle like a gem. But unlike my brother, my whole existence isn't ruled by some pussy—even if it is a fucking phenomenal experience, as he used to tell me.

"Did you miss me?" I say in a low voice. I don't know why I ask this because we were never close. I always kept her at a distance, no matter how much she tried to be nice to me or engage me in her world. Sister of Nate, once the crime lord around these parts, and a family who you needed to watch your back around unless you were part of their inner circle—I was not. She was always the woman that I wanted from afar but never would have gone there because of my brother. And now, she's the woman I hate—and have done for years. There is no room for anything in my heart except vengeance.

"Jax…" Her voice trails off again as I hover my lips by her ear, breathing in her scent and enjoying the uncertainty in her voice.

"Jax what?" I say, pushing my knee against her pussy a little more. I don't fail to notice the slight intake of breath from her.

"I'm sorry," she says, and I freeze, the words hitting me like a ton of bricks. Sorry. Such an easy word to say and one that changes nothing. But of all the things I expected to come from her mouth, it was never that.

"I didn't know they were going to kill him," she continues, her voice pained. "I didn't know…" The next thing I feel is her body shudder against mine and the wetness of her tears on my lips as they run down her cheeks.

My brows furrow. This isn't how it was supposed to go. There should be no crying, there should be no emotion right now other than rage from her as I haul her ass out of here and lock her away until I'm ready to end her life. That's what should be happening... and it isn't. Instead, I'm still stood behind her, still pushed up against her, still in shock that I've heard the word 'sorry' pass her lips, and still feeling her body shudder as she continues to cry silently.

I need to take her.

Why the fuck am I not taking her?

"If I could go back—"

"But you can't," I snap, clenching my jaw as I'm snapped out of whatever fucking state that just was, and then a knock at her office door has me muttering under my breath.

"Zoey, you in there?" comes the sound of a male voice from the other side of the door.

I quickly move and pull Zoey against me, my hand going around her throat, my other hand reaching for the gun tucked into the back of the waistband of my jeans, which I pull out and place against her temple.

"Not a fucking word," I growl as I haul her backwards. It's dark and I don't know the office well, but I know enough to know that there is a closet in the corner of the room. I quickly move until I feel my back connect with the closet, and then I turn Zoey to it and order her to open the door. She does without even putting up a fight, and then I push her in, making sure the door is closed behind me as we squeeze into the space. I have no idea what is in here, but I thank fuck that we were both able to fit as I push myself against her body, my hand going back to her throat, my face inches from hers in the dark.

The dark. A place I am friendly with and one that has comforted me for years. There is no place for light—only darkness in my world.

Seconds tick by that turn into minutes. I hear footsteps walking around. I prick my ears and am expecting Zoey to try and scream, lash out at me, anything to grab someone's attention. But she doesn't. She remains quiet whilst I hold her neck. She doesn't move except to breathe. This is definitely not the Zoey I remember. That Zoey used to fight no matter what. She would act and ask questions later. She would have a fucking plan in place before you even knew what was happening. She would never have just taken her fate quietly.

But this new Zoey? She's acting timid and like she's given up on life. She doesn't seem to have the same spark that she once did. I can tell all of this even though I haven't actually seen her face yet or seen the emotions that may flicker there. It's like she's beaten, and actually, that fucks me off even more. I wanted her to challenge me and make me realise that holding onto all of this anger for years has been for a fucking reason. Give me the excuse I need to end her life. But no. Nothing.

Frustration replaces my rage, and my thoughts are broken by a man speaking on the other side of the closet door.

"She's not in here... I'll go check the VIP area... Yes, I've tried to call her phone but there's no answer... Just find her..." I hear a loud sigh as my brain suddenly reminds me that I'm pushed up against Zoey... her breasts flush to my chest... her mouth inches from mine as her breath feathers over my face... if I were a lesser man, I'd be claiming her lips with mine in a heartbeat, but I'm not, and with my fingers wrapped around her throat, I am quickly catapulted back to what she's done.

Minutes tick by before I whisper in her ear, "Don't move." I turn and slowly open the closet door, my gun in my hand and ready to shoot if someone is still in here, but the room is in darkness once again, and I reach behind me, finding Zoey's arm and hauling her out of the closet.

I throw her in front of me and she tumbles to the floor.

Now is not the time to do anything other than give her a warning, so I lean over her, putting my face in front of hers. "This isn't over," I say before I stand up and make my way to the door, opening it slightly at first to check the coast is clear. It is, and then I'm walking out of there like nothing has happened, closing the door behind me.

---

"Where the fuck have you been?" Cole says as I walk into the bar—our bar, J's Place, the one that we might as well call home because we're here more often than not, and the one we named after Jason—a drink already being put in my hand. I take a glug before I put the drink back down and turn to look at him.

"Out," I say, sitting down on a bar stool and taking another swig of my drink.

"Don't get fucking smart with me, Jax," he says, and the way he says it has my hackles rising.

"Remember who you're talking to, fucker," I reply, my tone showing that he better not get up in my goddamn face. I run things here, not him—although he wants to.

He mutters under his breath before slapping his hand on the bar and walking away.

"Jackass," I say quietly, my focus going back to my beer once again. I rub my temple, feeling the impending headache that resides there. I saw Zoey fucking Knowles and I just left her where she was. Years of hatred, years of wanting revenge, vengeance, and I left her in her club. I mean, it would have been a ball ache to get her out of there, what with the place crawling with security and me being on my own and all that, so there's a valid reason, but it still pisses me off that she's not kneeling at my feet and begging for the fucking mercy that she doesn't deserve.

I feel a hand land on my back, and I turn to see that it is one of the bar regulars—Sonia. I almost groan out loud because this woman is a pain in my ass, always trying to get in my fucking pants despite me having zero interest in her. Don't get me wrong, she's pretty, but she's not my type. Her fake tits and lips do nothing for me, her peroxide blonde hair dry as fuck, and her makeup hiding any natural beauty that may be underneath. I prefer natural girls, makes it more believable—that and the fact that it doesn't feel like you're fucking a blow-up doll.

"You look stressed, baby… let me help you out," Sonia purrs as she runs her hand down my back, and I find myself swivelling around on the bar stool, my beer still in my hand.

"Sonia…" I begin, but an image of Zoey flashes in my mind as my trousers are unzipped and my cock is sprung from my boxers. I shouldn't do this, I shouldn't lead her on, but when the image of Zoey refuses to leave my mind—her curves, her face, everything the way I remember before my brother was killed—I find myself letting this little scenario play out.

Sonia's lips wrap around my dick, and she sinks down until I'm hitting the back of her throat. With my elbows resting on the bar, I look around and see a few patrons occupying booths on the other side of the room, but if they mind what's going on at the bar, they don't show it, and I'd tell them to fuck off out of here even if they did. This is my world. My rules. My playground, and fuck if anyone is going to tell me how to run it.

She starts to move up and down, and I take a swig of my beer before leaning back and trying to enjoy the show. The thing is, as much as she bobs up and down and as hard as she sucks, Sonia still does nothing for me. I mean, yeah, my dick is hard because who the hell wouldn't be with it stuck in someone's mouth, but as for getting off… yeah, that's the problem here.

She's devouring me like a fucking lollipop, and most guys would be well on their way to blowing their load, but I'm not even off the starting block. Shit.

I take a deep breath and another swig of my beer, telling myself to relax and literally blow off some steam. Seconds turn into minutes, and then minutes turn into what feels like fucking hours as she moans around me.

Should have just gone the fuck home, this is no use, I'm getting absolutely nowhere.

But then I see her, stood at the back of the bar, just inside the door, her eyes on me.

Zoey.

The fuck is she doing here?

Something inside of me stirs—something I don't want to stir.

She's hidden in the shadows, but I see the emotion in her eyes. She doesn't know what to make of this moment, and fuck if the way her lips are parted doesn't make me want to take my cock out of Sonia's mouth and stick it in hers instead. And I can do absolutely nothing to the reaction my body is having at seeing her here as I feel the build-up of my release starting.

I hold her gaze as she bites her bottom lip. I should go and get her, lock her up and make her suffer, but it's been a while since I orgasmed with anything other my hand and my cock doesn't want to give up now that it's finally enjoying the moment.

I hold Zoey's gaze as I move my hand to the back of Sonia's head and grip her hair, moving her up and down faster, harder. She makes more noise around my cock, but the only thing that grips my attention is stood across the bar, and even from here I can see her breathing quicken. Her hand is on the top button of her shirt as she plays with it, and I allow myself the fleeting thought of ripping her hand away and undoing that button myself before baring her breasts to me so I could taste her…

Fuck. I feel myself release into Sonia's mouth, hitting the back of her throat as she swallows every drop. And even when she's finished lapping me up and stands, all I do is watch the woman that I hate walk out the door, closing it quietly behind her. But I'm not ready for her to go yet, and I shove Sonia away from me as I button up my jeans and stalk after Zoey without a word to anyone. If Sonia is pissed off or hurt by my actions, I have no idea, and I couldn't give a fuck. There is only one target on my mind, and as I push the doors to the bar open, I see her about to get in her car. I quickly move, getting to her in a few strides and grabbing her arm, whirling her around and caging her against the car.

I take a moment, looking at her, my eyes tracing her face, her neck, and the curve of her breasts as she breathes heavy.

"Like what you saw?" I say, noting her flushed cheeks.

"I have no interest in who sucks your dick, Jax. Now get away from me," she says, but makes no move to push me away.

"When I'm ready." Intimidation is my forte, and I plan on intimidating the fuck out of her. "Why did you come here?" I ask.

"To talk."

I laugh, because we are so beyond fucking talking at this point. "Really? And what could we possibly have to talk about?"

"The past."

"Right. And you think this is going to fly with me because..." I let my voice trail off as I wait for her answer.

"Because I don't want to run anymore," she tells me, her eyes still holding mine. This is the Zoey I remember, the one who won't back down. This is the Zoey I used to be intrigued by, and fuck if this doesn't intrigue me all over again.

"Maybe you should have kept running, Zoey, because all I want to do is make your life a living hell," I tell her, but I omit saying that I also want to fuck her senseless, because who wouldn't? However gorgeous she is though, it doesn't matter, because I can see past the end of my dick—most of the time.

"This is my home too, Jax—"

"*Was.* It *was* your home," I bite out.

"It still is," she affirms, but I'll make her see that it isn't. She doesn't belong here.

"Kid yourself all you want, it won't matter soon, not once I've finished with you," I say as I run my nose down the side of her cheek and stop when my lips hover over hers. "Because you have no idea what you've done by coming back here, but I'm going to enjoy watching it play out."

I push away from her and round the car, but her voice has me turning back around to look at her. "I told you to do your worst, Jax. No need to be shy now."

"Oh, pretty girl, shy isn't even in my vocabulary."

"So come on then," she says, goading me, her arms stretched out either side of her. "I'm right here, so let's go."

I cock an eyebrow because most wouldn't be egging me on in this way. But Zoey? This is what I was waiting for, that fire, that spark.

"Not tonight," I say and turn back around. This isn't part of the plan, and I need to stick to the plan. I've already veered from it by going to her earlier, in her office, and I don't need to change it up any more than I already have.

"Pussy," I hear her say, and I stop in my tracks. I feel her behind me seconds later, her body so fucking close, her scent wafting around me, her fucking breath on the back of my neck. "That was one thing I never had you down as, Jax," she whispers. "A fucking pussy." I clench my hands into fists as I clench my jaw. "You told me this wasn't over, so prove it. Show me just what the big bad biker boy can do…"

And buttons pushed.

I turn, placing my hands on her hips as I lift her feet off the ground and move to her car, dropping her on the bonnet, making her lean back as my body covers hers.

"Don't fucking push me."

"Or what?" she says as she leans up and lightly runs her lips over mine. My dick twitches. Fucking hell.

"Patience," I tell her. "All good things come to those who wait—or bad, in your case."

"Well, don't keep me waiting too long," she purrs.

"Why ruin half the fun?" I say before I move off of her and walk back to the bar, because if I don't, then I'm going to bury my dick in her until she screams my name. And that is definitely not on my agenda when it comes to Zoey Knowles.

## Chapter Eight

### Zoey

I have no idea what came over me last night when I went to Jax's bar, but all I can think about is his body covering mine on that car bonnet and what could have happened but didn't.

I'm not here for this shit. I need to do what I came to do, not piss around with Jax in some game of cat and mouse.

It's hard to keep my mind occupied though as memories from the past assault me.

*"This is my brother, Jax," Jason says as they both sit at the bar.*

*"Nice to meet you, Jax," I say as I hold my hand out to shake his, but he makes no movement as he glares at me and grunts. "Jeez, he's friendly, huh?" I say to Jason, who chuckles.*

*"Yeah, he's the easier one of the two of us to get along with," he says sarcastically, but you can tell it's said with a lot of love too. Jason is nothing if not an open book, and Jax appears to be the polar opposite.*

*"Play nice," I hear Jason say as I bend down to grab two beers from the fridge.*

"Don't worry, Jase, I can handle him," I say with a wink as I place the beers in front of them. "On the house."

Jason thanks me and Jax just reaches for the bottle with a grunt. God, he's going to be a tough one to crack, but I am nothing if not persistent.

I can't fail to notice how good looking Jax is. I mean, Jason is hot, don't get me wrong, but there's something extra about Jax… maybe it's the way his eyes are that little bit harder, his persona a little bit darker, as if luring you to experience the darkness with him. Whatever it is, it's telling me to leave well alone, but I've never been very good at playing by the rules.

Jason goes to use the bathroom, leaving me alone with Jax.

"So, not a talker, huh?" I say as I lean my elbows on the bar in front of him. His eyes pierce mine, and dear God does it make my pussy tingle.

"Not really," he says, pretty much the first words he's spoken since sitting down.

"Small talk is no good then," I comment as I bring my hand up and tap my finger on my chin, as if in thought.

"No talk is good," he says, and I stop tapping my finger and stare at him. He has truly mesmerising eyes.

"Wow, okay, no talking… And let me take a wild guess, there is no Mrs Jax Jones either," I say.

"By choice," he affirms.

"Of course," I say with an eye roll, and I'm about to give up on this conversation and move away, but his hand finds its way around my wrist, his fingers locking in place as heat travels along my skin from his touch.

"All you need to know is not to fuck my brother over," he says in a low voice that does absolutely nothing to abate the excitement fluttering through me from this exchange.

"And you need to know that I don't take too kindly to threats," I say back, keeping my eyes level with his. I don't back down for anybody, and I'm not going to start now.

"Hmm," he mumbles. "This is going to be fun then, pretty girl."

The ding of my phone startles me, and I shake my head, pushing the memory to the back of my mind.

There has always been something about Jax, even that very first time, and I have a feeling like we're about to have the most intense game playing ever. I mean, he pushes, I push back. It's how it's always been, and it just comes naturally to me to act that way with him. I forgot how much I used to thrive on it.

I turn my attention to my phone, to see that Nate has text me to 'check in' as he calls it. I reply with a roll of my eyes.

***Zoey: I'm good, bro, stop worrying.***
***Nate: It's my job to worry.***
***Zoey: If I need you, I'll ask.***

I love my brother, I really do, but I can handle myself, and lord knows he's got enough security keeping an eye on me. I may not be able to see them, but I know that there are around, somewhere. Ronan has also been sweeping by daily since he couldn't find me in Purity a few nights ago. It's a little annoying but I get it, Nate's name still holds power here, regardless of him being gone. I haven't mentioned the little visit from Jax to anyone because they would have me locked away and handcuffed to one of them if I needed to go anywhere before I could blink. I can't cope with that. I came here for peace of mind, and I won't get it if they keep wrapping me up in cotton wool. That's why I went to Jax's bar the same night he paid me a visit. I wanted to talk to him, to make him see how much guilt I live with, because I think he needs it—he's still hurting too, that much was obvious even from our short exchange.

But then I got to his bar and watched that woman suck him off, and I don't even want to acknowledge how that made me feel. I refuse to.

However, I do need to speak with Jax at some point, but before I attempt to pull at that thread again, I'm visiting someone else first.

My feet move over the grass, making it crunch underneath my shoes as I go. My eyes seek out what I'm looking for—the grave of Jason Jones. I never said goodbye, and to me, it's imperative that I do that. I know that Jason wouldn't hold what happened against me, he wasn't that type of person—he was kind, and he would be telling me to move on and let go. But I can't, not yet.

I continue to walk through the rows of headstones in the direction I went the other day, when I saw the bikers all stood around, until I see one up ahead in the shape of a motorbike, and I know that it belongs to him. There's a plaque in front of the bike, and I make my way towards it, my heart starting to race. I shouldn't be getting so worked up but it's hard to stop the adrenaline, the fear, the guilt, the hope, and every other emotion possible from rushing through me. There are fresh flowers that have been put into pots at the bottom of the headstone—orange flowers, Jason's favourite colour. The bouquet that I carry in my hands seems to weigh a ton as I stand at the foot of his grave and just stare at it in silence.

The birds flutter around, chirping away as they happily go about their day whilst I stand there at a loss for words. I should have stayed to bury him. I should have been around to pay my respects and not skulk back here years later, expecting forgiveness.

I was a coward when I ran, and I'll forever hate myself for doing that. If only I could turn back the clock…

*"You'll have to catch me first," I shout as I run across the field behind my house, feeling freer than I have done in a long time, no security flanking me. I need this freedom, the joy that comes from not feeling like I'm*

trapped. It's why I need to speak to Nate about scaling the surveillance back for me, I need room to breathe.

I can hear his laughter as I run forwards until I hit the trees on the other side of the field. I quickly scramble over the fence that runs around the outside, and I disappear into the trees, my heart pumping as I go.

All I can hear is my footsteps crunching on the leaves beneath my feet, and I know that I need to be quiet or it's going to be easy for him to find me. I slow my pace, looking for a hiding place and finding one across the way, almost like a little cave. I move towards it and get on my knees to crawl inside, but just as I am about to disappear into the darkness, I feel a hand grab my ankle. I shriek in surprise and manage to turn myself around before his body lands on top of mine, caging me in as his hands come either side of my head.

"Gotcha," he says before he smashes his mouth against mine, igniting me from the inside, fuelling the desire that I harbour for him.

"You know," I say as he moves his lips to my neck and starts to nip lightly. "We are probably way too old to be running around like this."

"Who cares," Jason says, his lips now kissing along the edge of my vest top. "We had to grow up young, so let's just enjoy this moment of peace before we have to return to the real world and deal with all the shit that awaits us." He moves my tank top down, placing his lips over my lace bra, right where my nipple is. I arch my back as he sucks it into his mouth, a moan escaping me from his touch.

"We can't do this here," I whisper, but even I can hear how unconvincing I sound.

"There's no one around, no one to catch us…" he says before pulling the lace down with his teeth, exposing my breast completely.

"But…" The words die on my lips as his hand makes it way to my pussy, his fingers sliding past my knickers and finding my clit. "Oh God…"

I shake my head and feel the tears falling down my cheeks.

I need to get a hold of myself. I came here to say goodbye and I'm not leaving until I do.

I move to the side of the grave and then kneel down, lying the bouquet in front of the pots of flowers.

"That's a pretty cool ride you've got there," I say as I look at the headstone and smile through the tears that are still falling. "I'm so sorry this is the first time I'm seeing it." I take a deep breath and make myself say everything I should have already said.

"I know that if you were here, you'd probably be telling me off for living in the past, but I can't help it. I need closure, Jase, and I don't know how to get it… and I'm hoping you'll help me. Starting here seems like the right place." I look around me, no one else here visiting loved ones that have passed. It's quiet, eerie but peaceful as the clouds roll in overhead, indicating the rain that was forecast.

"I never meant for it to end the way it did… I didn't expect my brother, Lucas, to be involved—if I had known, I wouldn't have gone anywhere near the place, and I will forever regret asking you to come along with me. I should have let Nate deal with it all, but no, I had to charge on in there like I had it all figured out.

"I am ashamed of myself and my actions. I'm guilty of every single person dying that day. And I'm so fucking sorry that you believed in me and trusted me enough to follow me into a battle that had nothing to do with you whatsoever.

"I wish I could turn the clock back, Jase… I really really do…" My words fade off as sobs rack my body, and I let it all out. I clutch my stomach, the pain ripping through me. I tell him I'm sorry over and over again as the heavens open above me and the rain falls, hitting my back and drenching me within minutes.

"I promise I'll be a better person; I'll try to let go of my guilt, but it's hard. So so hard. I feel it clawing at me daily, just begging to drag me into the darkness that looms at the sides like a predator ready to swallow its prey. I don't know how to let go… tell me how to let go…"

I don't know how long I stay there before I get to my feet and take one last look at the grave before saying, "I'll come back again soon." I go to walk away, but I turn and run into a hard chest before I'm hauled to the side and slammed against a large tree, just beside Jason's grave.

His hand goes over my mouth before I can make a sound.

"The fuck are you doing here?" Jax rages at me, his eyes boring into me, anger across his face.

My answer is a mumbled response, because until he moves his hand, I can't say shit. He seems to get the memo and moves his hand from my mouth to my neck, curling his fingers around as he holds me in place.

"I just came to pay my respects," I tell him, and he scoffs.

"Five years too fucking late, Zoey." His reply shows the bitterness in his tone.

"I get that, Jax, but I'm here now and I'm trying," I say. "Unlike you."

"What is that supposed to mean?"

"Well, this is the second time you've had your hand around my throat, pinning me in place, and add in the fact that you told me that this isn't over and I shouldn't have come back, yada yada, I'm assuming you still want revenge for what happened," I deduce.

"Damn fucking straight I do," he snarls.

"Well, come on then, biker boy, do your fucking worst," I say as flames ignite inside of me.

We hold each other's gaze for a beat, a challenge in both

of our eyes. I came here to fucking fight for my freedom, and I'll be damned if Jax is going to change that.

"You don't want to see me at my worst, pretty girl," he says with a smirk, his voice low and filled with a warning that I have no intention of listening to.

"I'm not scared of you, Jax. Not by a long shot," I tell him, even as my heart flutters wildly in my chest.

He moves his head forward until his lips are by my ear and he whispers, "You fucking should be."

He drops a kiss on my cheek, his stubble grazing my skin, before he removes his hand from my throat and walks away. I turn my head and watch him as he goes.

Whatever is going on in his head, he can bring it on, because I'm ready to play.

---

"Yo, babes," Kayla says as she bounds into my office, startling me out of my daydream. "You coming to the main room tonight?"

"I will do shortly," I tell her, sipping the coffee that I made fuck knows how long ago, the coldness making it taste foreign on my tongue. I have never liked cold coffee.

"Okay, well, the hot ass biker dudes are in tonight, just to let you know," she says with a wink before she flounces out of my office and down the hallway that leads to the main room.

Biker dudes.

Jax.

Fuck.

My legs move me of their own accord until I'm in the bathroom that connects to my office, checking over my appearance and running my fingers through my hair. I'm pretty pleased I decided to wear my black leather trousers and white crop top that shows off my tan from living in the sunshine for years. Wait… What the fuck am I doing? Why do I care what I look like? I let out a breath and then make my way to the main room, a pull luring me there like nothing I've experienced before even as I question it.

Jax hates me, so why the fuck am I making my way to see if he's here? Another question I don't want to answer as I push the doors to the main room open and make my way inside. The bass of the music vibrates through me, the bar area packed, the dance floor crammed with people enjoying their night, and there, to my right, sat in the corner, is Jax and a couple of his biker crew. He's already looking at me, and I force myself to move to the bar, making my way to the staff latch so I can go behind and grab a drink. From cold coffee to something stronger… tequila, that always leaves a nice burn behind. I pour myself a shot and down it quickly, no lemon, no salt, just straight up. I want to feel it as it makes its way down my throat, and feel it I do, especially when I sink another two shots before leaving the main room altogether, avoiding Jax's gaze as I walk past. I could have gone the other way out of here, but for some reason, there is something inside of me that stirred the minute I saw Jax sat there. Something that has been dormant for so long and is coming to life more and more each time I see him.

I make my way to the VIP area, which is quieter, and I move to the back of the room, sitting down in the booth at the back that is reserved for anyone bearing the Knowles' name. It's also the only booth with a curtain for privacy. There's plenty of room in here for me to sit down, lean against the wall, and stretch my legs along the seat. I close my eyes and let my head drop back. I should go back to my office for privacy really, but... I've felt alone for so long, and I guess that even with a curtain blocking me from everyone's view, I don't feel quite so isolated. I always used to be the life and soul of the party, the one who had everyone up and dancing and laughing well into the night. How times have changed.

I listen to the sultry tones of the music in this room, a contrast to the dance music pumping away on the main floor. In here, it's more rhythm and blues to set the mood—it's sexy, and the girls that dance on the stage always have playlists ready to go.

I let the music take me away, until my eyes fly open at the sudden invasion of someone nudging my feet.

"Get the..." The words die on my lips as I see Jax stood there, one arm resting against the side of the booth and the other holding the curtain open. Dear God, he looks so good with his short dark hair all messy, his tank top showing off the tattoos that adorn his arms and the backs of his hands, and his muscles clearly on show. "What are you doing here?" I say as he invites himself in and closes the curtain behind him. "I asked you a question."

"And I'll answer you when I'm ready," he bites back, further fuelling the irritation that sprung up within me at the sight of him—along with something else... something that has me wanting him to... *No, Zoey, you don't want him. Fucking stop it.*

"You don't own this place, Jax," I say as he looks down at me, his arms crossing over his chest.

"Maybe not, but we have unfinished business."

Why is his voice making my skin tingle?

Why is the way he's looking at me making me want to climb up his body and lock my lips with his?

Shit.

"Unfinished business." I scoff. That's one way to put it.

"Don't you mean that you want to get back at me for what happened and you're here to make sure that happens?" I say icily, despite my core heating with every second he stands there.

He smirks before moving across the table from me and taking a seat, his arms leaning on the table as he pins me with his stare.

"Don't presume to know what I want, pretty girl," he says, his voice low and full of… wait… shouldn't he sound dangerous? Why does he sound anything but to my ears? Shouldn't I be feeling intimidated? Fuck no, I've dealt with bigger assholes than Jax Jones.

Before I can reply, the curtain opens and drinks are placed on the table by one of the bar staff. They swiftly leave and redraw the curtain across, leaving us alone once more. There is a bottle of tequila on the tray and two shot glasses. I look at Jax questioningly. He ignores my unanswered question and proceeds to pick up the bottle and open it, pouring two shots out and pushing one of the glasses in front of me.

"We're going to play a game," he says, picking his glass up and holding it between his fingers.

"A game? Aren't we playing one of those already?" I say with a raise of my eyebrows.

He smirks at me. "I figured we may as well have one moment of fun before I make your life hell until I decide to kill you," he states, so blasé, not batting an eyelid. But then, I don't bat an eyelid either. This isn't the first time I've been threatened, so if he thinks this shocks me, he's forgotten who I am—or is that, who I used to be? I guess I'm about to find out…

## Chapter Nine

### Jax

My plan was to come here and fuck with her a little bit, hence the tequila. And as much as that hate burns deep inside of me, I'm entitled to a bit of fun first… right?

"Here's what we're going to do," I say before my brain can think of more questions as to why I want to have fun with Zoey of all people—I mean, the top reason would be because she looks like every guy's wet dream right now, but that's by the by. "We'll each ask a question, yes or no answers only. If the answer is yes, then we drink the shot. If the answer is no, then the other person drinks the shot."

She snorts and crosses her arms over her chest.

"What's the matter, pretty girl? You worried you'll be drunk and unable to fend me off?" I goad her.

"Please, I'd need to black out completely in order to be unable to fend you off," she retorts as she squares her shoulders and leans her arms on the table, mimicking what I'm doing. "Let's go."

I knew it would wind her up… maybe I know her better than I think I do? *Stop that. You don't know her. All you know for certain is that she is reason your brother is dead, now stop fucking around.*

"You can go first," I offer.

"All right. She ponders her question for a second before she says, "Do you hate me?"

Surprisingly, a laugh leaves me as I down the shot and pour another one. "Bit of a low blow asking something like that," I say.

"I prefer to think of it as knowing your opponent and knowing how to crack them," she remarks, a smirk on her face.

I refrain from answering because it would only end in a slanging match, and I want to make sure she's pliant enough for when I get to the real nitty gritty questions.

"Are you happy to be back here?" I ask.

"What happens when the answer is yes and no?" she asks.

"Well, in that case, I guess we both drink," I say as I pick up my shot glass again.

"Yes and no it is," she replies before knocking her drink back at the same time I do. I refill the glasses and off we go again.

"Do you really want to kill me?" she asks, her eyes boring straight into mine.

I don't answer as I pick up my glass and knock my drink back.

"Wow," she breathes.

"Is there an issue here?"

"I knew you hated me, Jax, and yeah, earlier you said you wanted to kill me, but deep down, I just thought you were really really mad and that we'd work it out somehow," she admits, her eyes falling to the glass in front of her.

"Why on earth would you think that I wouldn't mean it?" I ask, suddenly a little uncomfortable with the direction this conversation is going.

"Because we were friends once," she almost whispers.

"We were not friends," I retort.

"As good as. Yeah, okay, we'd give each other shit most of the time, but I always thought that was just the way we were," she replies with a shrug.

"Maybe it was, but that was a long time ago, Zoey, and I've got years of hate that's built up inside of me," I tell her, being more open than I had planned, but fuck it, if this is our moment of truth, then so be it.

"I hate that you hate me," she says quietly—quiet enough that I could have missed it, but I don't. I heard her loud and clear, and I have no idea what to do with that.

"Did you love Jason?" I ask, going straight for the kill. Her eyes widen briefly before she schools her expression.

"That's a very broad question," she says, but really, it isn't—at least, I don't think it is.

"Not really. You either did or you didn't," I say as I shrug my shoulders.

"I cared for him deeply," she says, her eyes dropping to the table.

"That's not a yes or no answer."

"It's the best one I can give."

"Let me change it then," I say as she looks back to me. "Were you *in* love with him?"

The seconds tick by. I need to know whether my brother died knowing she loved him or whether he died because she gave him the magical pussy and kept him dangling from a hook for her convenience.

"You better drink your shot," she says, and I see red. My hand flies across the table and is around her neck, my body following as I climb over the table and pin her to the seat.

"You bitch. He fucking loved you," I say, my nose almost touching hers.

"And I loved him, I just wasn't *in* love with him." She doesn't look scared as I hold her there, and she doesn't try to fight me off either. The slight spark of the old Zoey I saw when I first rocked up to this booth has gone, only to be replaced by this shell of a woman that I once knew.

"He fucking died for you," I roar.

"I know, and I fucking hate myself for it, but I can't tell you I was in love with him because I wasn't! I cared for him, loved him as a friend, and yes, it could have been so much more, but it was cut short because of one stupid decision that will haunt me for the rest of my life, so don't think I haven't suffered, Jax. I have felt guilt every fucking day since, probably more so seeing as I know he was in love with me and I didn't have the chance to return that love to him," she shouts back, and there's that spark again, it's there, hovering away in the background. "You can get in my face and yell at me all you like, but for fuck's sake, either try to kill me or move the fuck on."

"Move on? Move on? How dare you," I grit out. "You ran the minute he died, Zoey. You left me to pick up the pieces and bury him. You didn't even stick around to say goodbye. Who the fuck does that?"

She looks confused for a second, but I can think of nothing but the anger burning through me.

"What are you talking about? You wanted me here?"

"Of course I fucking did," I say before I can stop myself, not thinking about what I'm saying.

"Why? You just said we weren't friends before, so why the fuck would you have wanted me here?" she asks.

"Because you knew him as well as I did. You spent more time with him in the last few months before his death than I did. You spent more time with me…" I stop myself, my brain catching up to my mouth, finally. I can feel my body shaking and I drop my hand from her throat and turn away from her, needing to regroup.

"Jax…" she says, and I feel her hand on the top of my arm, her fingers wrapping around as she squeezes gently. "Talk to me, and I mean really talk to me."

"I can't." I don't turn and face her because I fucking can't. I need to keep hating her. I need to hold on to that or the last five years of my life have been totally unjustified.

"Jax, please…" Her voice cracks and I can't stay here anymore. I have to go. I have to get out. Seeing her again has fucked with my emotions more than I care to admit.

I shrug her hand off of me and I pull the curtain back, stalking out of the booth and across the room until I'm outside and on my bike, heading back home.

## Chapter Ten

### Zoey

No way. Nuh uh. He doesn't get to walk away from me like that.

I quickly make my way outside and hear the roar of his bike in the distance. Fuck it.

I run back inside the club and grab my car keys from my office before I high-tail it out of there, somehow avoiding security as I do. Good, I don't want them following me or interfering. And luckily for me, I learnt a long time ago how to dislodge the tracker that they put on my car, so once I'm out of here, they won't be able to locate me. It's dangerous, yes, but if what comes next means the end of my life, then so fucking be it. I make my own damn decisions in this world. You get one life to live, and I've been throwing mine away, buried in grief and regret… but no more. Jax has ignited a fire inside of me, and I guess that answers my earlier question too… the old Zoey is still inside, she's just been hidden for so long that I forgot she still existed.

I rev the car and quickly pull out of the car park and onto the main road. I see security clock me as I go past, but by the time they inform Ronan and someone gets to their car, it'll be too late, and I'll be well on my way to Jax's place—my instincts tell me that's where he's gone, so that's where I'm headed.

I speed along the roads, knowing the way to his off by heart. Jason lived with him, and I spent a lot of time there once Jason and I became a 'thing', but I block Jason from my mind and focus solely on Jax.

I need him to tell me what that mindfuck of a conversation was back there, and if it will help him with his grief in the process, then great. I think it'll help me too, to be honest. It's the most alive I've felt in years.

I turn into the road that leads to his place and race my way down his long-ass driveway. The house is set a fair way back from the road and he has no neighbours, preferring to have his privacy, as I once heard him say.

I see him getting off his bike as I screech to a stop in front of him, gravel shooting out from underneath the tyres as I do. I pop the door open and get out, slamming the car door behind me before making my way towards him. He has a pissed off look on his face, but I don't care. Good. Maybe it'll make him talk to me more. His anger seemed to make him more loose lipped in Purity, so I'll push his buttons until he cracks.

"What the fuck was that?" I shout. "Storming off like a goddamn toddler."

"You shouldn't be here," he growls as I come to a stop in front of him.

"No way, you're not doing that," I say as I waggle my

finger in his face. "You can't just growl at me and expect me to go after what just happened in the club."

"Nothing happened," he says as he turns his back on me and starts to walk to his farmhouse. It's bloody huge, but that is not my focus right now.

"Yes it did. If it hadn't then you wouldn't have run off," I say, and he stops and whirls around.

"Run off? I didn't fucking run anywhere," he says through gritted teeth.

"You couldn't get out of there fast enough when your idea of fun took a different turn," I say, not backing down.

"Fun? Nothing about this is fun," he shouts, taking a step closer to me. "I thought you coming back here would solve this hatred inside of me. I thought it would give me my fucking life back when I finally ended yours, but all its done is fuck with me more."

"How? I don't understand this, Jax—" But my words are cut off as he grabs me and hits my back against the wall of his house, knocking the breath out of me for a moment.

We're both quiet. Both breathing heavy. Both locked in some sort of trance as everything around me disappears—there is only him.

"You... you..." he starts, but his voice trails off, and my frustration begins to return.

"Christ's sake, Jax, what is it that you're trying to tell me?"

"This," he says, and then his lips crash against mine, hungry, feral, like he hasn't feasted in decades. And I return it. I should be pushing him away. Why aren't I pushing him away? But I block those thoughts from my mind as his tongue invades my mouth and tangles with mine. Oh holy fuck.

I grab his hair as he kisses me, and he growls into my mouth, causing a thrill to run right through me. I lift my legs and wrap them around him, pulling his body closer. His hands move to my thighs, and he digs his fingers into my skin as he moves me away from the wall and starts walking us to fuck knows where. I'm too in this moment of madness to give a fuck about anything other than his lips on mine.

I feel him lift his foot and then a door slams open. We're moving again, up some stairs, and then I'm being thrown onto a soft surface—his bed. There is an animalistic look in his eyes as he starts to undress before me, until he's there in nothing but his boxer shorts. I bite my bottom lip and then he growls, "Get up."

My body complies before my brain can think about it and I stand to the side of the bed.

He prowls towards me and says in a low voice, "Take it all off."

Shit. Am I really going to do this? Am I really going to cross whatever line this is and get naked for him? Apparently so as my hands go to the bottom of my top and pull it over my head and then undo my trousers, sliding them down my legs, before unhooking my bra and throwing it at him. It hits his chest, and he looks at it as it falls, my eyes following the movement and clocking the size of his cock currently tenting his boxers.

His eyes roam back up me, devouring every inch of my skin. Good grief, my skin is tingling. I've had sex before, I've felt the stirrings of my body when I've gotten naked with a man, but never in my life have I felt anything like this… and I don't even know what *this* is. I can't explain it as adrenaline and excitement surges through me. But I do know I've lost my fucking mind and the guy that wanted to kill me not half an hour ago is currently pushing those boxers down his legs and letting them fall to the floor, freeing his cock.

"Get on the bed," he says, and I take a moment to really think about what the hell I'm doing here... but that moment doesn't last as he clearly doesn't have any patience, pushing me down until I'm led flat before disappearing from view. I prop myself up on my elbows, wondering if this has all been some big joke, but then I see him crouched at the end of the bed, his hands landing on my thighs and pushing my legs apart before his tongue lands on my pussy, licking me through my lace knickers.

I cry out as his eyes connect with mine, and when his fingers move and rip my knickers off me in one go, I think I'm about to come right there. Never have I ever had my knickers ripped off of me, and I have to say, it's pretty hot—okay, a lot hot.

He then moves his thumbs and parts me, opening me up to him, and I drop my head back as his tongue flicks my clit. He flicks it over and over, and my arms give out as they tremble, but then he stops and I prop myself back up quickly, wondering where his mouth went.

"Eyes. Give me your eyes or I stop," he says before he returns to my clit and lavishes attention on it, his eyes holding mine. I struggle to stop my eyes from closing, I struggle to hold myself up, I struggle to fucking breathe as his lips close around me and he sucks, hard.

"Jax," I say as I sit up more until I'm balancing on my ass, his face still buried in my pussy and my hands gripped in his hair.

"Ride my face, pretty girl," he growls against me, and I do. I rock against him, needing more. And I guess he reads my mind because he pushes two fingers inside of me and I ride them at the same time as I ride his face.

His other hand reaches up and pinches my nipple, and I

scream as I come all over him. I come hard and fast as he doesn't let up, still sucking, licking and working me into a frenzy that threatens to make me pass out.

I grip his hair harder, almost hard enough to pull it out, and then when I can take no more, I collapse back on the bed, but then I'm being flipped over, and my knees are being bent so my ass is in the air. He slaps me once across the ass cheek before plunging his dick inside me. I arch my back, feeling him hit me oh-so-fucking deep.

He rides me as hard as I rode his face. There's nothing gentle about this fuck. It's bruising, feral, as his fingers dig back into my thighs hard enough that I know it will leave marks.

He pounds into me over and over again, and my hands grip the edge to stop me flying over the side. Dear God, this man knows how to fuck.

I push back into him, meeting his thrusts just as hard, and then he roars as he reaches his release. I clamp my walls around him and ride his dick until he stops, and we both collapse onto the bed in a hot and sweaty mess.

I shut my eyes for a second whilst I try to compose myself to get up and walk out of here, but I feel the pull of keeping my eyes closed calling to me. It's late and I've been fucked harder than I ever have been in my life. Just five minutes won't hurt…

## Chapter Eleven

### Jax

I wake up and stretch before opening my eyes, the sunlight blaring in my room and already pissing me off as it disturbed my sleep. And then my eyes shoot open as I sit up in bed, my mind remembering what happened last night. But when I look beside me, the bed is empty, and when I check the room for any signs of her, I see that her clothes have gone.

Probably a good thing, seeing as I hate that awkward morning after bullshit—nice fuck, now off you go, and all that. Except, that wasn't just a nice fuck, it was the most mind-blowing fuck I've ever had. And it just had to be with Zoey Knowles. Shit.

I get out of bed and go to the bathroom to take a piss and chuck some water on my face before pulling on a pair of joggers and making my way down to the kitchen. I need a hit of coffee before I even think about starting the day and wrapping my head around what last night means—if it means anything at all.

I make my drink and sit at the table, remembering every little detail of how I was inside of Zoey. Her curves, the feel of her, her heat, her taste... oh her fucking taste. I guess she does have a magical pussy after all. The thought makes me chuckle, and then I stop myself because I'm an idiot who tasted what was once his brother's. Does it make me a traitor? Does it mean I've forgotten why he died?

I gulp down my hot coffee and run my hands through my hair. Instead of trying to work my way through the clusterfuck of questions assaulting me, I'll go to the bar and see what the guys are up to and what business needs taking care of. Of course Ronan and co still run the streets, but we don't just sit by and wait for shit to happen. We have things to take care of too, and it's been a few days since I checked in, so it's about time I showed my face and occupied my mind.

I clap Cole on the back as I walk in. "How's things?" I ask as I sit on the stool next to him.

"You'd know if you'd bothered to come around in the last couple of days," he replies sarcastically.

"Had shit to take care of."

"Like what?" he asks.

"Like my dick," I say with a smirk.

"Whatever, dude." He takes a sip of his beer and I note that he's drinking at ten in the fucking morning.

"Why are you drinking so early?" I ask, because yes, there are occasions when a beer is needed earlier than normal, but those occasions are usually fucking stressful, so if there is any stress to be had, I want to know about it.

"Shanice," he says, and there is no further explanation needed. Shanice is his ex, and all she does is give him shit.

"What does she want this time?"

"What do you think?"

Money. It's always money.

"You know you don't owe her shit, Cole," I tell him.

"I know, but she just gets under my skin, you know?" Yes, yes I do know.

"Kev out the back?" I ask him, and he nods his head as he stares back into his pint glass. I clap him again on the back and then head for the door that leads to the back room. I know Cole hates that he fucked around behind her back, but he's got to let that shit go at some point and stop feeling so guilty. It happened two years ago, and she still has her claws in him. At some point, you have to move on.

I stop for a second. Move on. Huh. Funny, I could take my own advice at this point, but I'll throw that to the back of my mind with all the other Zoey-related shit for now.

"What have you got for me, Kev?" I say as I enter the kitchen at the back and see Kev eating breakfast. A full English. My stomach growls.

"There's one in the oven keeping warm, my man," he tells me, and I quickly go to the oven, pick up a tea towel and take the plate out. I go to the table and sit opposite Kev, quickly digging in because hot sex makes me fucking ravenous, apparently.

"You wanna chew or just inhale it all?" Kev says a few minutes later when I'm halfway through the plate. I look up at the guy who women say is a Jason Momoa lookalike, to see he's smirking. "So, who is she?"

"Who is who?"

"The woman you fucked last night who is making you eat like that," he clarifies.

"No one important," I muffle around a piece of toast, a pang of guilt hitting me. "Anyway, back to the question I asked when I first came in. What have you got for me?"

"You need to let off some aggression?" he says, and I nod my head a little.

"Something like that."

"Well, you know we've been keeping tabs on the Yates family?"

"Of course I fucking know, we've been on this shit for months," I tell him, as if he's lost his mind and doesn't remember the stakeouts we've done together and the countless hours spent trying to find a way into their fold.

"Last night, they moved out. All of them. Gone."

"Gone? What do you mean gone?" I ask as I drop the toast I was eating on the plate.

"Disappeared."

"They take anything with them?"

"Not that I can see."

"I guess that means we're looking for clues as to who fucked with our operation and then we'll be paying them a visit."

"You guess right, my man," he says, smiling. Kev loves a bit of detective work, and I love to give people what they're due, so it makes us the perfect team for this job.

"Hurry up and eat your food so we can get out of here," I tell him as I stand up and take my empty plate to the sink, swilling it off before putting it in the dishwasher. What can I say? I may be a moody fucker, but I'm domesticated.

## Chapter Twelve

### Zoey

"Hey, Ronan," I say as he walks into my office. I've very quickly gotten back into the swing of things since being back here, and there's a part of me that missed running my club for five years.

"Where were you last night?" he asks me, sitting in the chair on the other side of my desk.

"Out."

"Out? You know that answer isn't going to fly, Zozo," he tells me, and I stop what I'm doing and look up at him.

"Ronan, I appreciate you've been looking out for me since I've been back, but you're not my brother and you have no right to keep tabs on me."

"He might not be, but I am," a voice says—a voice I know very well—before they step inside my office with a smirk on their face.

"Nate? What the hell are you doing here?" I ask, absolutely stunned that he's stood across from me right now.

"I thought I'd come back for a visit," he says with a shrug of his shoulders.

"Visit my ass," I mutter as Ronan gets up and shakes Nate's hand, clapping him on the back at the same time in that macho way that men do. "And where are Kat and Gracie?"

"At the house," Nate says, as if them flying halfway around the world to come here for a surprise visit is totally expected.

"Uh huh, and you're here for how long exactly?" I ask, crossing my arms over my chest and tapping my foot on the floor.

"Not sure. As long as we feel like."

"And what about Gracie needing to be at school—you know, that place she started at like two weeks ago?"

"What's with all the questions? Aren't you pleased to see me?" Nate says, holding his hands out either side of him.

I roll my eyes and don't even try to stop the smile that makes its way across my face as I go to him and give him a hug. "Of course I am, it's just a shock, that's all. And if you're here just to check up on me, then you needn't have bothered because I'm perfectly fine."

"I can see that," he says as he smiles at me. "Anyway, dinner at our house tonight, seven p.m."

"Wait… you're here for a visit but you're inviting me for dinner?"

"Sure. Gracie can't wait to see her Auntie Zoey," he says, and I laugh at the fucker.

"Well played, bro," I say as I go back to my desk and sit down. "Now, if that's all, you can both leave."

"Charming," Ronan says as he goes to the office door, Nate following behind him.

I turn my attention back to the papers on my desk, when Nate says, "Oh, and we'll be talking about where the hell you were last night over dinner." And then he's gone, closing my office door behind him.

Bugger.

---

I have had Gracie attached to my hip for the last half an hour. She's clearly missed her Auntie Zoey, and I have to admit that I'm glad they're here. Coming here alone hasn't exactly gotten rid of my guilt and the demons that still haunt me from all those years ago, and having family around reminds me that I need to push past what I have been struggling with and finally move on with my life.

"So, tell me," I start as I sit down at the dining table and place Gracie in the chair next to me. "Why did Nate really want to come back?" I ask Kat as she busies herself placing food on the table. It's quarter to seven and Nate is yet to materialise, and I'm guessing he's still with Ronan.

"You know what he's like, Zoey," Kat says with a sigh. "He was never going to relax with you halfway across the world, so here we are." She doesn't even try to sugar coat it, and I love that about her. Kat won't bullshit me, and for that she has had my respect since day one.

"But Gracie has just started school—"

"And a couple more weeks of not being in school won't hurt her. Besides, we brought a tutor with us, so she doesn't miss out on anything."

"You're shitting me," I say, and then my eyes widen as I hear Gracie say, "Auntie Zoey!" Talk about a face palm moment.

"Sorry, baby girl," I tell her as Kat shakes her head and brings more food over to the table. Gracie hops down from her chair and leaves the room without saying another word, but a few seconds later, she's back, holding a jar out towards me. "Pound for the jar."

"Seriously?" I say in disbelief.

"Oh, she's serious," Kat says with a chuckle. "She heard Nate say a naughty word the other day and now we have a jar."

I find myself smiling as I dig deep in my pocket for a coin but only have a five-pound note. "No change, Gracie," I say with a shrug of my shoulders.

"That's okay, Auntie Zoey, the five pounds will do." And with that, she takes the five-pound note from me and pops it into the jar. My mouth drops open as she runs from the room and past Nate, who is walking into the kitchen.

"Whoa, slow down, pumpkin," he says as she races down the hallway. "What's got Gracie running out of here like her ass is on fire?" he asks as he walks over to Kat and places a kiss on her cheek.

"She just scored some money for the swear jar," Kat tells him.

"Yeah, and made interest on the payment without even trying," I finish. "I had no change, so she took the whole note from me."

"That's my girl," Nate says, and we all burst out laughing. God, I've missed them so much. "This all looks delicious," Nate says as he sits down and grabs a warm bread roll from the basket. Gracie re-joins us, minus the jar, and we all dish ourselves up some food and then we chat comfortably about what's been happening since I've been back here, and my fretting about being questioned over where I was last night disappears from my mind, that is until Nate excuses Gracie from the table so she can go and play with her toys and turns to me and says, "So, who were you with last night?"

Bugger. I should have known. And I still don't have an answer because there is no way I am telling him I was with Jax.

I roll my eyes and spoon the last part of my dessert into my mouth. Kat smirks behind the glass of water she's bringing to her lips, and I narrow my eyes on her—in an affectionate way, of course.

"I was busy and it's none of your concern," I say when I swallow my mouthful and pick up my glass of wine, taking a few sips, knowing I'll need more than the one glass if he carries on questioning me.

"Nice try but that won't work," he says.

"Nate, for fuck's sake, I am an adult, and I don't need you questioning me over what I do," I tell him, my irritation rocketing. "Is that all you came here to do? Question me?"

"Zoey, stop overreacting—"

"I am not overreacting," I interrupt.

"You kind of are," Kat says, still bloody smirking.

"Don't you start," I say, turning to look at her briefly. She puts her glass down and holds her hands up as if in surrender, but I know she likes to fuck with me, and vice versa. It's how we are, and the only reason I'm so annoyed is because of Jax. I mean, Nate questioning me is annoying as hell, but that's just who he is and who he always will be. It's in his nature, and I guess being back on his old playing field will have him more on alert than usual. Nate isn't the problem here, I know that, but I have no idea what to tell him, so I blurt out the first thing that comes to mind.

"If you must know, I had a one-night stand."

Kat can't help the snigger that leaves her, and Nate looks like he'd rather have been told anything else.

"Christ's sake," he says as he picks up his beer and takes a swig.

"See? It's not always such a good idea to question everything," Kat says, amusement in her tone.

"I'll deal with you later," he says to Kat, and I cringe when she quietly says, "I'll look forward to it."

Ugh.

I know they love each other but for fuck's sake.

"Now, if you're done questioning me, I am going to Purity," I say as I stand and push my chair back a little aggressively, making the legs scrape loudly on the floor.

"Zoey," Nate says as I reach the doorway.

"What?" I say as I whirl around.

"Be careful," he says on a sigh, and I scoff.

"Of course, rule one-oh-one of the Crime Lord Handbook—always be careful and trust no one, right?"

And with that, I march my way along the hall and fling open the front door, slamming it behind me.

I shouldn't be so pissed with Nate but he's an easy target for my frustration because he's my brother and I know he won't hold it against me. And of course, I will apologise later, but right now, I just need a minute. My head is full of Jax, and I need to deal with what that means sooner rather than later. But first, tequila is on my mind.

# Chapter Thirteen

## Jax

I've been watching the Yates' house for the last few hours, just to see if there was the possibility of any comings and goings, but there's been nothing. Not a fucking peep. And I'm pissed off that I've wasted my time when I should have just gone in there in the fucking first place.

I rise from my hiding spot in the woods, just to the side of the property, and I beckon for Kev to follow. He's a few feet behind me, crouched behind a different tree, and when he stands, I turn my focus back to the front door of the house. It's a pretty decent place—painted window frames that match the light green colour of the door, flowers in pots either side, lining the three steps that take you to the front door, and the yard is tidy with just a few rogue leaves scattered across the driveway. Hard to think that a family that deals in trafficking women would live in such a quaint place. I mean, sure, it's way back from the main road and seemingly buried in a load of trees, but you always imagine traffickers to live in a shitty apartment that's run down and is just a place to rest their head at night whilst they wait for their dealer to show up with their next fix. That is very rarely the case though when it comes to shit like this. It's usually some fucker in a suit that you wouldn't suspect.

The Yates family were the catchers, the ones who would reel the women in and then bundle them off to whatever hell awaited them. And we were so fucking close to having our moment and taking out the top dog, and now… well, now it's all been shot to shit because someone couldn't keep their nose out.

I walk up to the front door, turn the doorknob and push it open to be greeted by silence—as expected. I make my way inside, keeping alert and pulling my gun from the back of the waistband of my jeans. I can hear Kev behind me, but I don't turn around to see what he's doing—all I need to know is that he has my back and I have his. So rarely can you find others to trust in this world, but he is one of the few that has nearly taken a bullet for me on a couple of occasions, and in my book that equals total trust.

I sweep the rooms to the left and hear Kev sweeping the ones to the right before we make our way upstairs. We move quickly but quietly, checking the rooms as we go along, and its only when we get to the last room that we get the shock of our fucking lives.

"Thank Christ for that, I thought I'd be stuck here all fucking night. I mean, there's waiting it out and scouting, and there's just being fucking ridiculous."

I don't react on the outside, but on the inside, I am questioning why Ronan is sat here, looking smug as shit.

"You knew we were out there?" Kev asks, and I grit my

teeth. We're always careful not to be seen or detected unless we want to be, and this fucker just outsmarted us.

"Of course I knew," Ronan says, and then scoffs. "This isn't child's play, Kev."

"Why are you here?" I boom out, finding my voice.

"You think the Yates family disappeared for no reason?" he says, and I resist the urge to call him a motherfucker, because of course Ronan interfered—it's what he does, and has done on a few other occasions, and it's annoying as hell.

"Should have guessed," I mutter.

"Yeah, well, you know nothing goes down around here without me knowing about it," he remarks.

*What about how I fucked Zoey and made her scream? Know about that, do you? Yeah, I think not.* Oh how I'd love to throw that little titbit in his face, but I won't, because to admit it out loud would be to acknowledge that I fucked my dead brother's girl. Yeah, not something I'm proud of, and right now it's something I can push to the back of my mind—mostly. I haven't had sex like that since… well… ever… *Now is not the fucking time, Jax, put it to bed.*

"So, here's the deal. I can give you the Yates', but I need the top name," Ronan says, and I smirk.

"You don't know who's running the show?" I ask.

"I have an idea, but I want confirmation."

"Is that so?" I say, and now it's my turn to feel a little smug.

"We both want the same thing here—for all of them to suffer and be eradicated from existence. So, let's not fuck about. Name," he demands.

"Don't talk to me like I'm one of your fucking minions," I boom, my eyes narrowing slightly. "You encroached on what we were doing, not the other way around."

"Oh please, you don't think I gave the go-ahead for you to do this?" Ronan remarks, and I feel my hackles rise further.

"The fuck you talking about?" I question. "I run the show and I don't ask anyone for shit."

"That's not strictly true…" Ronan says, pausing for a beat. "You might wanna have a word with Cole before you go thinking that you… how did you put it? 'Run the show,'" he says sarcastically.

"Cole?" I can't help but wonder what the fuck I've missed because Cole doesn't know how to run anything other than his mouth. And then it hits me… the way I wanted to leave this alone because I was focused on finding Zoey, but then Cole convinced me this would be a good way to occupy my time for a while because I needed a break from looking for her. "Motherfuck."

"Maybe your crew isn't as in order as you think?" Ronan says, and I swear to God, I could easily punch this fucker. I look forward to the day I get to do that, but I need to keep my cool right now. Yes, I want to be the one to rule the streets without him in the picture, but he holds so much fucking power that I need to chip away at—soon. The walls built around the Knowles' empire are so fucking high that I'm going to need to scale my way in, and pounding on the guy that runs it all isn't the way to go… or so I've been told. Maybe I should just do it and take my chances?

My guys keep warning me not to do anything drastic, and my head has been so full of what happened to Jason that I've been distracted, but I'm quickly getting fed of being blocked from doing what I want to do. It's clear that I need to go and question Cole, because it seems he's taken my trust for granted and worked behind my back. This is why Cole doesn't make decisions, because he's an idiot that doesn't think things through, and now we're all going to pay the price for his stupidity.

"Name, Jax, now," Ronan says, and I feel Kev step up beside me.

"Give it to him," Kev says quietly, but I know Ronan hears him.

"And if I do that and confirm whatever the fuck you think you know, what do I get, other than the chance to fuck up the Yates'? I mean, it's gotta be worth more than a little rough and tumble with scum, right?" I keep my eyes locked to Ronan's, not backing down. He doesn't scare me, and he knows it.

"You want money? Status? To be untouchable?" he questions.

"I'm already untouchable, asshole," I grit out.

"Yeah, so it seems," he ponders with a questioning look in his eyes that I have no desire to decipher.

"What I want is something you won't ever give," I tell him.

"You don't know if you don't ask."

"I'm not asking you for shit." I can't ask for what I want because it would never be allowed. Ever.

"Then just give me the name and we'll call it quits."

I turn on my heel and give him my back, and as I walk towards the door, I throw the name of the top dog over my shoulder. "Julian Smart."

I make my way back outside and start the walk back to where we left the bikes a few miles away.

"What the fuck, dude?" Kev says as he falls into step beside me. I walk briskly, needing to get the fuck out of here. "Why did you just give up the name like that? Why didn't you ask for a deal?"

"Because what I want, he can't give me, I already said that

back there," I tell him, keeping my eyes firmly trained on the track ahead of us.

"And what the hell is it that you want?"

"Zoey."

"Zoey? What do you mean, Zoey?"

"I mean, I want her and I'm going to fucking take her."

"Jax, no—"

"This isn't up for debate, Kev. I'm taking her, and that's final."

"For fuck's sake, Jax, don't you think you need to be done with this shit already?" Kev says, and this time, I stop and turn to him. My blood is heating beneath my skin, and I can feel the anger working its way through my body.

"This shit?" I bark. "No one understands. No fucking one, and I get it, I do, but so God help me, if you don't have my back right now then I'll take your fucking head off, regardless of the respect I have for you." I'm deadly serious, and he knows it.

"I've always got your back, brother, but this will start a whole world of shit. Are you ready for that?" he asks.

I have no hesitation as I reply, "I've been ready for the last five years, don't make me wait any longer."

## Chapter Fourteen

### Zoey

Tequila always makes the world seem like a better place. I've got that numbing feeling that comes from the several shots I've consumed. I pick up the bottle and pour myself another—I don't have the patience to keep walking to the bar, so I took the bottle to save myself the hassle.

I'm sat in the corner of the VIP bar, hidden in darkness, my back resting against the glass window that looks out over the town below as I face the stage and wait for the next act to come on. I don't make a habit of watching the women that dance here—unless they're auditioning, of course—but there's something calming about watching them work the pole. I mean, I can appreciate a woman's form and not want to do anything about it. The way they move, how they command the room, and how the men in here wish they could just have five minutes with them in a dark room.

I sink my shot and pour another as the lights dim on the

stage and the music starts to play—a sexy bass ringing out, announcing the start of the next act.

I watch as the spotlights turn a dark red and a figure appears in the middle of the stage, on her knees, with her head bowed so we can't see her face. The lights stay low as she begins to move to the beat, working the stage like the pro she is—and probably giving every man in here a boner in the process.

I'm totally zoned out to everything else as I relax and enjoy the buzz of the tequila… that is until I feel a hand slide around my throat and lips tickle the shell of my ear as they say, "It's just me, pretty girl."

My heart races more from those words than they did from the hand going around my throat.

"Enjoying the show?" he says as I attempt to move before his fingers grip a little harder and his other hand moves to my chest, holding me back in the chair.

I am aware that no one can see us in this corner, not unless they physically move and peek around the wall—it's why I sat here in the first place, to be left alone, which I no longer am because bloody Jax clearly felt the need to encroach on my personal space. And the horrifying part is that I don't really want to fight him off of me, even though I absolutely should. I've been trying to forget about the other night, in his bed, with his dick inside of me and his tongue teasing my pussy… but it turns out, hate sex is clearly the way to go, because fuck did he rock my world and leave me wanting more.

"What are you doing here?" I ask, my eyes moving to look at his hand resting on my chest.

"I just thought I'd come and pay my favourite lady a visit," he says, his lips still by my ear, his breath feathering over my skin.

"Favourite lady," I say, and then I scoff, because I am so far from his favourite lady it's ridiculous.

"And then I saw you sitting, on your own, and well, it seemed too good an opportunity not to walk on over here," he says, ignoring my sarcasm at his 'favourite lady' comment.

"What do you want, Jax?" I ask, and then he moves the hand that's around my throat and grips my chin as he turns my head so I'm looking at him.

"You," he says before he smashes his lips to mine. What the fuck? Even as I question what the hell is going on, I open my mouth to him, letting his tongue tangle with mine. He tastes so fucking good, and I'm so fucking weak right now.

Am I dreaming?

Is this some kind of tequila haze that I've found myself in?

But as I feel his hand on my chest move and slide inside my top and under my bra until his fingers are pinching my nipple, I quickly deduce that I am not dreaming and this is happening... in my club... whilst I sit here and enjoy every single fucking second of what he's doing.

This is the first time I've seen him since the night at his place, and I really didn't expect it to go down like this, but I'm way too buzzed from the alcohol to think any of this through rationally.

He rips his mouth away from mine and turns my head back towards the stage, where the dancer is gyrating provocatively on a chair. My head is locked in place as Jax's other hand moves away from my nipple and out of my top and snakes its way down to the waistband of my skirt.

"So glad to see you wore a skirt, pretty girl. It's going to make this so much easier," he whispers, and goosebumps erupt all over my skin. Fuck. The way he talks to me, the way he calls me 'pretty girl', and the way he makes me feel is sending every one of my senses into overdrive. All I can think about is him. All I want is him. All I feel is him. The list is fucking endless, and there isn't anything I can do to stop my body's reaction to him as his fingers move down to my thigh and then disappear under my skirt until they are brushing my pussy, which is already wet for him.

"Already soaked for me," he says, and then he licks along the shell of my ear, and I shiver. "Open wider." And I do, moving my legs apart more so he can do whatever the hell it is he wants to me, because I don't care about anything other than what he's doing.

He slides one finger past my knickers and finds my clit, which he starts to rub in small circles, slowly. My head falls back and lands on his shoulder, and then his lips are on my neck as he works me into a frenzy where I'm dying for him to go faster but needing him to keep this going for as long as possible because I'm pretty sure this is what heaven feels like. And I don't give one single fuck that I am in the VIP section of my club, because that's what I'm starting to realise happens when Jax is around—nothing matters.

I let out a low moan as he moves his finger faster and his teeth nip my neck.

"Jax…" My voice trails off as our eyes finally connect and we hold each other's stare.

"Show me what I do to you, pretty girl."

And I'm completely lost to him as I stare into his dark brown pools. His eyes are the key to his soul, and I can see something hidden in the depths, but I'm not sure what it is, and then he pushes on my clit harder, moves his finger even faster, and then he's covering his mouth with mine to swallow the moans that erupt from me as I come hard and fast on his hand.

Oh. My. God.

He doesn't move his mouth from mine until my orgasm is over, his tongue massaging against mine softly, gently. I don't understand any of what is happening right now, but I know that I want it. I want whatever this is to continue, because fuck me, the way he brings me to orgasm is like nothing else I've ever experienced.

When he removes his lips from mine, he takes his hand out of my knickers, brings his fingers to his lips, and then he puts them in his mouth. If any other man did that, I'd probably want to die on the spot, but with Jax it's just… hot.

"So, did you just come here to get me off or was there another reason?" I say when I've gathered myself somewhat, my voice all breathy and shit.

"I just came here to remind you that you're mine," he says, and I'm about to question him on his statement, but he's up and out of here as quick as he showed up, leaving me to ask myself for what feels like the millionth time… *what the fuck?*

---

Fucking Jax. He totally came in and bulldozed on my quiet moment, and now I'm leaving Purity because the buzz from the tequila has worn off and all I seem to have a buzz from is him. I've tried to push him from my mind since I came back here, but it's no use. He's in there, and he's not going anywhere anytime soon.

I wave goodbye to Ronan as I walk out the front doors and head for the car that is waiting for me—there is always a car waiting for me and it's fucking annoying, but on this occasion, it's needed, seeing as I've consumed too much alcohol to drive. I don't even take any notice of the driver as he opens the door for me to climb in. I realise it's rude, but I'm usually polite, so I'm hoping it'll give me a free pass. Then again, I don't really give a shit at the moment. I came back here to sort my head out, but all I am doing is messing it up more. I mean, it's Jax, for fuck's sake. Why did I let him get me off in my own damn club? Or better yet, how could I have let myself fall into bed with him in the first place? It's wrong on so many levels, but then why does it feel so right when he's near me and when he puts his hands on me?

Ugh.

The car door shuts behind me and the driver gets in the front, and then we're off, heading back to my house. I stare out of the window as the streetlights rush past—seems the driver wants to get me home rather quick tonight, maybe he's had enough for one day too? The streets are quiet as we go, but seeing as it's two in the morning, I guess most partygoers are either still in the club, going home to get laid, or going home alone and depressed—like me.

God, I hate how whiny I'm becoming. This isn't me. I'm a fucking Knowles and I need to start acting like one. I want to be the girl that used to be the life and soul. I want to be the girl that lets her hair down and doesn't always think of the consequences because she's too busy enjoying life. I want to be the girl that gets the guy. The one who will hold her when she cries and make her feel like a goddess between the sheets. The guy that you can argue with passionately and then fuck like you hate one another but really you couldn't imagine your life without them. I want that. I could have had that…

"Enough, Zoey," I say out loud to myself. "It's enough," I whisper as my eyes focus back on the streets whizzing past—streets I no longer recognise. In my hazy tequila fog, I sit forward, my eyes squinting as I try to make out where the hell we are, because it sure as shit isn't the way to my house.

"Um, excuse me," I say to the driver, but I am greeted with silence. "Hey." I try again but still no reply. "I think you took a wrong turn…" My voice fades off as we make a left turn down a lane which is lined with trees either side, and my gut starts to churn. Shit. This isn't good.

Where the fuck are we going?

I feel around for my handbag, but of course, I didn't bring one. I don't ever really need to carry a bag with me because I'm always surrounded by security, especially at the club. And my phone is still sat on my desk back in my office. Double fuck. *Stupid, stupid Zoey.*

I was so wrapped up in the aftermath of Jax that I totally forgot about my mobile. Great. Come back here to sort myself out, and now I'm in this car with God knows who.

*Okay, just breathe, you've been through enough shit previously to be able to deal with whatever this is.*

Clear your mind.

Stay alert.

Focus on any little detail that may help you get out of this situation in one piece.

I train my eyes outside the window as the car slows and eventually pulls to a stop. I can see nothing but trees surrounding us, and the thought crosses my mind that I am in a very real-life horror movie. You know, the ones where the woman gets dragged to a cabin and is made to do shit she doesn't want to do before the beast that took her there eventually kills her after she's endured so much depravity that she welcomes the angel of death.

*Jesus Christ, Zoey, get a grip.*

I watch as the driver opens his car door and gets out. Now

I really wish I had taken notice of his face back at Purity, because I can't see fuck all in the dark, other than his outline.

He opens my door and grunts at me, "Get out."

Here we go. Do or die.

I slowly move my legs to the side and step out of the car, rising to my full height, and then I'm quickly yanked by my arm towards the man in question as he turns me, so my back is to his front, his arm coming across my chest to lock me against him.

"Don't try anything, just do as I say and you'll be fine," he says as he lets me go and nudges me forwards. "Walk."

That's my only instruction. Walk. So I do. I walk and walk through so many goddamn trees, until I see a cabin in the distance. Oh fucking hell no… it *is* a scene from a horror film.

I need to get away from this asshole, whoever he may be, but I see no way out. I could run but he'd probably catch me pretty damn quick, seeing as I'm wearing heels and he's probably used to doing this shit. It doesn't strike me as his first rodeo.

I can't go in that cabin… if I do, I don't know if I'll ever come out.

Fuck it, I'm going to try and make a break for it.

As we keep moving, I notice that you have to walk over a small bridge in order to cross a river flowing just down from where the cabin is situated on a small hill. This could work…

I reach the bridge and step on it, waiting for my moment.

One.

Two.

Three.

I whirl around when I'm in the middle and crouch down, kicking my leg out and hooking it around the guy's ankle. He doesn't see it coming and his legs swing out from underneath him. He lands with a loud bump as I kick off my heels and get to my feet. My mind is in overdrive as I tower over him and raise my foot, bringing it down on his dick, and he howls in pain. That's my cue to run.

I run so fucking fast I think my legs might fall off, and I swear to God, I have never sobered up so quickly in my entire life.

I am aware that my feet are crunching on the leaves that have fallen on the ground, but my only focus is to get to that car. I've hotwired cars previously, so it's no biggie. In fact, it was one of the first things Nate showed me when we were younger—not your typical brother and sister thing but it's come in handy over the years.

I stay focused and keep moving, getting closer and closer to my mark, and when I see the car in the distance, I almost slow down and let out a sigh of relief. But there is no time to stop. In this world, you only have seconds to make a choice. Seconds where anything could happen, and valuable time could be lost. I don't intend to lose.

I push my body harder, my lungs screaming at me to give them a break, but my adrenaline forces me to keep going. Not going to lie, having a crime lord for a brother has certainly helped somewhat—shame I was an idiot in the first place and didn't get my phone or check who the fucking driver was though. Rookie mistake, and one I won't make again. Living away from here and on an island far away has made me far too complacent.

I am a few feet from the car, and I am convinced that a hand is going to shoot out and grab me before I get there, but it doesn't, and as I yank the car door open and climb inside, locking the doors behind me, I get to work on hot-wiring my way out of here. I'm clearly going to be over the drinking and driving limit, even if I do feel sober, but needs must right now.

"Come on, you son of a bitch," I curse, as it takes longer than I wanted to start the damn car, but then the purr of the engine infiltrates my ears and I look up to see that the guy is running towards me. I allow myself a small smirk as I rev the engine and put the car in reverse.

"So long, asshole," I say, and then I floor it. The car shoots backwards, but this isn't my first time at reversing to get out of a sticky situation, and I manoeuvre to a place where I can turn. I spin the wheel and the car does a quick one-eighty, and then I'm off, leaving the guy trailing after me and eating my fucking dust.

I breathe a sigh of relief as I emerge from wherever this lane is and make a right turn, back the way we came. I'm going to have to wing it somewhat because I was so zoned out for most of the ride, but all that matters is putting as much distance between me and whoever it is back there.

## Chapter Fifteen

### Ronan

"Search every single camera," I instruct the security team.

"Yes, boss," they say in unison as they quickly scatter to go and find where the hell Zoey has gone. It was only when one of my guys was patrolling out the back that they saw Zoey's driver unconscious on the ground, and it was brought to our attention that something had gone seriously wrong. I saw her walk out of here three hours ago, she even waved at me for fuck's sake, and I pray that nothing has happened to her.

I run my hand over my face and through my hair as I try to stop my mind from thinking of the what ifs. But it's no use, I know this world and I know that more sinister than good lurks around every corner. And it's with a sigh that I put my hand in my pocket and grab my phone, pulling it out, ready to make a phone call that I really don't want to make.

I unlock the screen and scroll down my list of numbers until I find Nate's name. He's going to lose his shit. He's been back for a matter of forty-eight hours and now his sister has gone missing. Brilliant. Some people would say I'm overreacting, but like I said, sinister over good and all that.

I dial his number and wait as it rings out once, twice, and then a third time before he picks up.

"What is it?" Nate barks down the phone.

"Getting slow in your old age," I joke, but I realise precious seconds are being wasted and I can't afford to waste them, so I continue with, "Zoey's missing."

"Jesus Christ. I'm on my way," he says before the phone goes dead. He doesn't need to ask where I am because he already knows that I won't be leaving Purity until I have a reason to go and look for her. He'll also know that I have eyes on her house too. He trained me well. I can do my job to the highest standard, but if I'm honest, I fucking miss him being here. Nate is like the brother I never had, and when he left, I took all the responsibility gladly because he saved me years ago and I will forever respect him for that—not to mention he lost his right-hand man, Stefan, during the whole Lucas and Jessica debacle. Grim times, but we've all had to move on and adapt—Nate just did that by taking his family somewhere safe, and I can't say that I blame him. But now, he's back, even if it is for a short period of time, and I kind of wish he was staying.

With a shake of my head, I make my way to Zoey's office and round her desk, sitting down in her office chair and eyeing her phone for what feels like the millionth time. I'm furious that she didn't take it, and I used to always tell her to just keep it on her even if she didn't use the damn thing. I even joked about putting a fucking chip under her skin, and I tell you, it isn't so much of a joke now.

I sigh and bring up the cameras on her computer screen, clicking to earlier in the evening when she walked past me and left the club. Since she's been back, I can see she's plagued by something—and my best guess would be grief, but I'm not certain. I mean, she left here with no closure, no goodbyes, no nothing after what went down with Lucas and Jessica. I don't know how she's been coping, because for the last five years, all I've really had is the odd text message from her, and that's just been a short response when I've asked how she is. We used to be quite close, always messing around—she was like my best female friend—and I've missed her too.

I need to make this right. It's my duty as the leader of the streets to make sure things run smoothly and that my house is in order. It's what I am trusted to do.

I closely watch the cameras out the front as she leaves. Her car is waiting, as it always is, but the driver keeps their face shielded from sight—their head bowed low, their shirt collar pulled up, and the cap on their head angled correctly to avoid any hint of recognition their face may spark. I zoom in but I can't get anything. I scour their body for anything redeeming, like a hump on their back or some shit, but nothing. I already know I won't find anything because it's about the tenth time I've checked the damn cameras, and I can't even check the tracker on her car because it's been disabled. This guy knew what he was doing and had done his homework. Pisses me off that whoever this is has manged to sidestep every security detail I put in place.

"Ronan," I hear barked from the hallway, and I look up to see Nate stalking his way towards me.

"Cameras have been checked and there is no clear angle. The tracker on the car has been disabled, and Zoey left her phone here," I say as I hold up the phone, wishing for the millionth time that she had just taken it with her. Nate comes to a stop in front of the desk, his hand running over his face and a look of desperation marring him.

"Why the fuck did I ever think her coming back here was a good idea?" he mutters. "This is why I took my family away, because danger lurks around every fucking corner here."

Some may think that Nate had gone soft when he hightailed it out of here like his ass was on fire, but that isn't the case. I know he lived and breathed this world for years, until family took centre stage and ruled over everything he had ever accomplished. And given the chance, I would probably have done the same thing in his shoes. I also know it wasn't an easy decision to walk away, but he's kept tabs all the time he's been gone and advised me when I've needed it, so really, he didn't completely bow out of the fold, he just gave up being here in person to protect those he loved more than life itself.

"Who is the threat?" he asks me, and I hate that my response is, "I don't know."

He slams his hands on the desk and then paces the room. "De ja fucking vu," he mutters. "The last time I didn't know, look what happened." He stops pacing and looks at me with a murderous glare in his eyes.

"I know," I say quietly. "We'll find her."

"Yes we fucking will."

"Cameras are ready for you to go through," I say, because I know he'll want to check them for himself.

"You sure you haven't missed anything?" he questions as he rounds the desk.

"Positive."

He stares at the screen, at the blown-up image which is paused to show the dark figure that we are now hunting, and then he surprises the shit out of me by saying, "Then I trust your judgement. Let's go." And then I'm following him down the hallway and out to his car, with him and me barking orders to the team that are still here as we go.

We get outside and I jump into the passenger seat of his car, and then we're screeching away from the club and going in the direction the car went. I have no idea where we're going, but I'm waiting for my guys to ring me to tell me they have followed where the car went and give us the coordinates.

"It's been a long time," I mutter as we race down the road.

"It has."

"Do you miss it?" I ask.

"Sometimes." And I leave the conversation at that as we travel in silence, hoping by some miracle we come across Zoey, and praying to God that she is still in one piece.

# Chapter Sixteen

## Zoey

I was doing great—so fucking great that I was putting distance between myself and the asshole who tried to kidnap me, and then bam… I felt like I had been hit by a fucking arctic lorry, and I blacked out, but now I'm coming around as my head feels like it's going to explode with pain.

I clutch my head and close my eyes again, trying to regulate my breathing and get some coherent thoughts. I try to clear my mind and process what happened to make me feel like death.

Headlights in the middle of the road.

Lights flashing and blinding me.

The swerve of the steering wheel.

The car veering off the road and entering a field.

A sudden impact of my car being jerked forward with force.

My head falling and hitting the steering wheel.

And then darkness.

Not much to go on really.

Fuck.

I inhale and exhale slowly, and I open my eyes gradually. I'm led on my back, and my eyes fix on the ceiling fan above. The room appears to be bathed in dim lighting, and the blankets I'm led on start to feel itchy.

I slowly prop myself up on my elbows and look around. The room is sparse with only the bed I'm led on, a small cabinet to the right of me, a lamp in the corner, and not much else. Not even a window, just a vent in the corner of the room.

Where the fuck am I?

I look to the cabinet beside me and see a bottle of water, along with some type of tablets—just two next to the bottle. I am not fucking taking those, but I check the bottle of water to make sure the seal hasn't been broken, and when I see that it hasn't, I open it and chug it all down. Tastes like the best fucking water ever.

I groan as the thumping in my head continues, and I'm tempted to swallow the damn tablets waiting for me, but with no idea of what they are or who put them there, I will just have to try and work through the pain. I push into a sitting position and move my legs to the side, so they dangle off the bed. My shoes have been placed on the floor and I'm still fully clothed, which I am fucking grateful for.

I gingerly push to my feet and sway a little, putting my hands out either side of me to try and steady myself. It takes a few seconds, but I manage to stay upright, and then I walk towards the door, resting my forehead against the cool wood when I get there. Just a moment… I just need a moment…

Turns out, I needed more than a fucking moment, as I wake to find myself back on the bed.

What? How? Who? But my internal questions are quickly answered by the person clearing their throat from the corner of the room. I squint as I whip my head to the side too quickly, and the pain throbs once again as everything goes a little hazy. Jesus Christ, have I got a concussion?

"Just relax, pretty girl."

Mother of fuck.

I open my eyes so damn fast and am met with Jax's chocolate brown pools.

"What's going on?" I say as I sit up and prop myself against the headboard, drawing my legs up until I am clasping my hands around my knees.

"You're hurt and you need to rest. You're in no condition to—"

"Cut the shit, Jax. Where the fuck am I and what am I doing here?" I say angrily.

"Not really the way you should be speaking to someone who saved your fucking life," he growls back at me, and I frown. Saved my life? What? There are too many 'what's' floating in my mind right now.

"I saw you swerve off the road, and I saw that truck ram into your car."

Huh, so I did remember correctly then.

"I happened to be tying up some loose ends over the other side of town, which evidently worked out well for you."

"Worked out well for me," I say with a scoff.

"Well it did. If I hadn't been there then God knows what

would have happened to you," he says sternly. "You were unconscious, so after I knocked the two fuckers out that were ramming your car, I bundled them in the back and used the gaffer tape and rope they conveniently had in their trunk to make sure they couldn't go anywhere, and then I rescued you from the carnage that was your car and got you the hell away from there."

"And why is it that everywhere I turn, there you are?" I question, because he's just always fucking there.

He scoffs. "You really think that after all these years and after all of the searching I've done that I wouldn't have eyes on you at all times?" he says, and I realise that Jax is never going to let me escape the past.

"Oh my God," I say as I bring my hand to my mouth. I feel sick. No, wait, I'm actually going to be sick.

"Bucket on the floor by the bed," Jax says as he points to it. I quickly grab the bucket and empty whatever was left in my stomach. Lovely.

"You're probably feeling sick from the bang to the head, so I'll go clean that out and let you get some rest," he says as he comes over and reaches to take the bucket from me, but I stop him because I have so many questions I need the answers to.

"Wait… you can't just go," I say as I lock my eyes with him, feeling fucking pathetic.

"You're in no fit state to talk, Zoey. Get some more rest," he orders as he takes the bucket off of me and walks around the bed, heading for the door.

"Jax Jones, don't you dare walk out and leave me here without answers," I berate as I struggle to get off the bed.

"For fuck's sake, woman, just stay in the damn bed and we'll talk another time."

"No."

"Yes."

"NO," I yell, even as it hurts my head, and Jax curses before putting the bucket on the floor and coming over to me. He's towering above me, and his hand lands on my chest as he pushes me back down on the bed. He leans over me, his face so close, both of his hands now on my arms as he stares at me intently.

"Don't make me tie you down," he warns.

"Pfft."

He raises an eyebrow at me, and I hate that I like that little quirk he has. Ugh, the frustratingly handsome bastard.

"Don't test me, pretty girl," he says as he lets go of my arms and stands tall before turning and walking back to the door. "Take the tablets, they're painkillers, and get some more rest." And then he's gone, taking my sick bucket with him. I let out a groan of frustration and roll onto my side, my back to the doorway. I don't want to sleep but everything still feels fuzzy. What I really want to do is get the hell out of wherever this is and go home, but it seems my body betrays me as it listens to Jax's words, and my eyes slowly start to close.

## Chapter Seventeen

### Jax

"This is a bad fucking idea, man," Kev says as I come back up from the basement.

"I told you that you either had my back or you didn't," I say as I make my way over to the sink in the corner of the kitchen and wash out the bucket she just threw up in.

"I do have your back, but Jesus Christ, Jax, do you have a fucking death wish? Nate will kill you, he will kill you dead, and that's after he's tortured you and all of us for holding his sister hostage."

"She doesn't know she's being held hostage yet," I inform him.

"Minor details. It doesn't change the fact that we are all in danger," he continues, and I slam the bucket into the sink and turn to face him.

"I am not scared of some fucking crime lord, and if you are then you shouldn't be in this goddamn crew."

"I'm not scared either, but I am telling you that people will die all for the sake of a piece of pussy laying downstairs—" His words are cut off as I shoot across the room and ram him into the wall, putting my arm across his throat.

"Say that again, I dare you," I goad him, but he shakes his head. "That is more than just some piece of pussy down there." I point in the direction of the basement that lurks beneath the bar we own and conduct most of our meetings in.

"Jax, brother, look at what this is doing to you," Kev says as he moves his eyes to my arm that is still against his throat but not cutting the air off. And then it's like I wake up as I drop my arm and move back.

"Fuck," I say as I run my hands through my hair and stalk my way out to the bar to get a drink. The place doesn't open for another hour, so it's just me and Kev here at the moment, but the rest of the crew will show up shortly, along with the bar staff and patrons that will sit in here for the rest of the night, hoping to get a screw at the end of it.

I pour myself a shot of vodka and down it, feeling the burn travel down my throat.

"Dude, you need to take a minute and chill the fuck out," Kev says as he sits on a stool on the opposite side of the bar. I bend down and grab him a bottle of beer out of the fridge, opening it and passing it to him without a word. "You've been holding onto this anger for so damn long... it's not healthy, brother."

"I know," I say with a sigh as my shoulders sag with something like defeat. "I fucking know, but it's all I have left of him."

"No it isn't. It's all you've left yourself with, there's a difference."

"Stop," I say as I pour another shot and gulp it down. "I'm not here for a dear diary moment."

"Well maybe you fucking need one," he retorts, and if he weren't my closest friend here, I'd knock him the fuck out.

I glare at him, my nostrils flaring, and then the door to the bar opens and in strolls Cole, like he hasn't got a care in the world. I see red as he approaches the bar, and before I can think about what I'm doing, I lunge across the bar and grab him by the collar of his shirt.

"What the hell, man?" he says as he stumbles forward, and his chest hits the bar. Kev doesn't attempt to move, and neither does Shorty—birth name Sid, but he's always gone by his nickname that reflects that he's pint-sized compared to the rest of us.

"You walked in at the wrong time, asshole," I say as I grit my teeth in his face. "You think you can go behind our backs and make a deal with fucking Ronan?"

And there it is, the guilt written all over his face and his skin paling because I know.

"Yeah, that's right, you shook hands with him and let him run the goddamn show," I snarl. I let go of him and round the bar so fast that I'm behind him and whirling him around to face me before he can even blink. "Why the fuck would you do that? Why would you break the code and betray us by going to him?"

"I needed… I just…"

"Now is not the time to fucking stutter," I say as I bring my fist back and sock him straight in the stomach. Feels good to let some rage out, and it's his own fault for making himself a target.

"Jax, please, mate—"

"I am not your fucking mate," I roar. "I am the goddamn leader of this pack, and no one gets away with breaking the code."

I bring my arm back so I can punch him in the gut again, but I stop when he says, "I needed to pay the bitch off."

I feel the tension in the room dial down a notch and I look to Kev who just shrugs his shoulders at me. And then I look back to Cole who has a pleading look in his teary eyes. Fuck.

"Christ, Cole, why didn't you come to me? To us?" I say, slightly less irate than a few minutes ago.

"Because it was too much fucking money."

"How much?"

"Half a million."

"Jesus," I say on a breath.

"It was the only way to get her out of my life, man. She was driving me crazy, making me drink, and I was losing my shit."

I know he was, and I get that he was desperate, but half a million? That's outrageous. "You're a goddamn fool, Cole. You know that once she's snorted and drank all that money away, she'll be back, don't you?" I tell him, because he's really gone and done it now.

"She won't, I made sure to let her know this was it."

"Oh yeah, and I'm sure she got the memo for the cash, and she'll forget all about your little talk with her when she's broke as fuck and down in the gutter once again," I say sarcastically. He may have done the dirty on her and felt bad about it, but this bitch is nuts—psycho nuts to still be fucking with him like this after so much time has passed. I see him gulp, and I'm guessing he feels real stupid right now, but I can't let the fact that he went behind our backs go. It's not how we do things, and he knows it.

"How long?" he asks.

"Six months," I tell him, and he stares at me with wide eyes.

"Six months? Please, Jax, this is all I have," he says as he holds his arms out either side of him. "You guys are my family—my fucking lifeline. I can't be ousted for six months."

"You can and you are. It's a small price to pay considering I've beaten fuck out of people for less," I tell him, my jaw clenched.

"Kev, come on, man," he says as he turns his attention away from me, desperation in his voice. Kev stays silent, keeping his arms resting on the bar as he stares straight ahead, not even turning to look at Cole, and sips his beer.

"Shorty?" Cole says, looking over my shoulder, but all I hear is silence.

"Keep your nose clean, do your stint, and then we'll see about the possibility of you being brought back in," I tell him, crossing my arms over my chest and standing tall.

Cole's head drops and he pushes off the bar, walking past me and then Shorty until he reaches the door and looks back. "I know what I did was wrong and I'm sorry for that, but you know this will kill me, so I'll see you in hell, brothers." And then he leaves, the door closing behind him and the silence ricocheting off the walls.

"Was that necessary?" Kev asks, and I pin him with my stare.

"This is why you couldn't run things, Kev, you're too fucking soft," I say as I reach out and ruffle his hair. He bats my hand away and I chuckle—the first real chuckle I've had in days.

Despite ousting one of my guys, it is fucking necessary, no matter what the others think. They know the rules, and they know that things could have been a hell of a lot different to what just happened. I gave Cole a chance—a chance to change his future and put things right. And I will continue to ignore the fact that I should be doing the same thing.

## Chapter Eighteen

### Zoey

"Jax Jones, get your fucking ass down here," I shout as I stand behind the door that is locked. I've had enough of being stuck in this room, and I have a goddamn right to be let out of here, not to mention I need a fucking piss. Not very ladylike, I know, so sue me.

I hammer on the door until I finally hear what sounds like a bolt and chains before the click of a lock being undone, and I stand back, waiting for it to open. When it does, I charge at Jax, my hands out in front of me as they land on his chest, and I put every ounce of strength into pushing him backwards. But alas, the man is like stone, and he doesn't even budge. Bugger it. I revert to pounding on his chest with my fists, fury taking over every thought. And then I hear him laugh. Yes, he laughs at me, so I do the only thing I can think of, and I lift my knee and bring it up to his dick. Safe to say, his laughing stops as he lets out a grunt and his hands drop to his knackers as he bends over slightly.

Ha. That'll teach him to be so bloody smug.

"What did you do that for?" he says as he wheezes, and I smile at him.

"Because I am sick of being in this goddamn room, locked up like an animal."

"I see you took the painkillers then?" he comments.

"Yes, and I feel much better, so get out of my way before I knee you in the bollocks again."

"No can do, pretty girl," he says as he clenches his jaw and moves towards me, his hands moving to the tops of my arms, his fingers digging in as he walks me backwards to the bed.

"Get off of me," I say as I struggle against him. "I want to go home."

"Stop acting like a bloody child with a tantrum problem," he comments as he pushes me down on the bed and lands on top of me.

"You really want me to inflict more pain on your nuts, don't you?" I say as I try to wriggle my legs underneath him, but really, what's the point? He's like a flipping giant led on top of me. "You have to get off of me."

"No can do, not when you're being a raging bitch."

"Fine, I'll pee all over you then," I say with a sickly-sweet smile, and he rolls his eyes and groans.

"Women," he mutters as he gets off of me and hauls me up by my arm, marching me out of the room and across the hallway, pushing me inside a little cubicle and turning the light on. The door shuts in my face, and I huff out a breath. Great, not even a window in here, just another sodding vent.

I quickly pee and wash my hands, using the raggedy ass towel to dry them after. Ugh. This place needs a makeover.

I bang on the door and it opens, Jax once again escorting me like a doll that he hates back to the room I've been in for…
"How long have I been here?" I ask as he all but throws me inside and steps in, closing the door behind him.

"Not long."

"And how long is not long?"

"Two days."

"Two days?" I screech. "Jax, my brother will be doing his nut."

"Yes, he is."

"So then let me go."

"No."

"No? What do you mean, no?" I ask incredulously. And how can I not have had the urge to pee for that long? How is that even possible?

"I told you that you belong to me," he says, his eyes blazing with his words.

"Jax, I am not in the mood for this," I say with a sigh. "I just want to go home, let everyone know I'm okay and take a long, hot bath."

"Keep dreaming, pretty girl, because that isn't going to happen."

"Why?" I don't understand any of this.

"Because if your brother is going through even a sliver of what I have been through, then it's not enough. If you think that you can just come back here and act as if nothing happened five years ago, then you're sadly mistaken. If you could even feel an ounce of the pain that I have been through, then it still isn't enough."

I stare at him, totally blindsided by this turn of events, and then it hits me.

"You really do hate me, don't you?" I whisper. Even with

everything that has happened since I've been back, he truly fucking hates me.

"You have no fucking idea," he says, and my heart sinks.

"Jax…" My voice trails off, because I don't know what to say.

"What? Did you think that just because I fucked you and got you off that things would be different now? Did you really think that I could let all of that resentment go because you let me stick my dick in your pussy?"

"Of course not."

"Then how did you see all of this playing out, Zoey? Hmm?"

"I didn't," I say as tears start to form in my eyes, clouding my vision as I look down at my hands in my lap.

"No, because you never think, do you? As long as pretty little Zoey gets her way, then to hell with everyone else."

"Stop," I whisper as the first tear falls.

"What Zoey wants, Zoey gets, and to hell with the consequences," he continues.

"Please stop."

"I lost my brother because of you," he shouts. "I lost my only family member because you wanted to go on some act of fucking bravery to prove what exactly? Because if memory serves me correctly, you still needed your brother to save your ass. You couldn't do it. You didn't do your homework, and you had no real clue about what you were walking into."

"Oh God," I say on a breath as my anxiety increases.

"And you didn't even have the fucking patience to wait for me to be there too," he says, and my head flies up to look at him. He's breathing heavy, his nostrils flaring. And then I see something more in his eyes—pain, regret. I did more damage to him than I did to myself on that fateful day, and I never even knew it until this moment, because I ran away.

I say the only words I can think to say right now. "I'm sorry."

He scoffs. "Sorry doesn't fucking cut it." And then he turns, opens the door, and leaves, sliding the lock into place and bolting me in this room that feels like it's closing in on me.

## Chapter Nineteen

### Jax

I bolt the door to the room I'm keeping her in and slide down it until my ass hits the floor.

I'm losing my mind.

Having her back here is fucking with me more than when she was gone.

I thought seeing her again and putting my revenge plan into action would help me heal, give me closure, but so far, all I've done is make a mess of things.

I've fucked her, had the best sex of my life with her—and it was only the once with me hating her, so God knows what it would be like if I actually liked her—rescued her from a car wreck, and now I've got her locked in the basement room underneath the bar. Brilliant.

I know that Nate and Ronan are doing everything they can to find her, but it's pretty hard to find a trail when I destroyed any evidence that related to her going missing. I even got my hacker, Dev, to wipe any trace of her on the street cameras within a five-mile radius of where she ran her car off the road. Yes, I do my job thoroughly, but what is the outcome of all of this? It was supposed to be so her brother would suffer, so she would suffer and feel an ounce of the mourning I've been through, but I'm not sure that's what I'm accomplishing here.

"You okay, brother?" I hear Kev say, and I look up to see him at the top of the stairs. I push myself to my feet and shake my head—I need to stop this pity party for one.

"Peachy," I reply as I square my shoulders and make my way up the stairs. "Make sure no one goes down there," I say when I reach the top, and then I move past him and into the bar, heading for the front door.

"Where you running off too, sugar?" Tammy, the local whore, says, putting her hand on my arm to stop me.

"Don't fucking touch me," I growl at her before pushing the door open and walking into the night air.

I breathe it in, tilting my head to look up at the stars twinkling above.

"If only you were here, Jase," I say quietly. He would know what to do. In fact, if he were here then none of this would be happening.

I need to expel some of this frustration, and the only way I can do that is to inflict pain. Serious pain.

I walk to my motorbike and hook my leg over, sitting down and starting the engine, listening to the sound of it purring underneath me. I see Kev come outside the bar, and I pull off, screeching away from him and heading towards my destination with only one thing in mind—destruction.

My fist rams into the side of his face and I watch as the blood spurts from his mouth, flying across the floor. I hit him again, and this time, a tooth clinks against the concrete, landing right beside the chair he's tied to.

"You had one fucking job," I fume, my voice gruff and the blood beneath my skin boiling with anger that this bastard messed up.

"For fuck's sake, Jax, cut it out, will you?" Clint says between breaths.

"All you had to do was get her to the house, and you couldn't even do that," I say, rage consuming me.

"The bitch got away—"

I cut the fucker off by throwing another punch to the other side of his face, and then I ram my boot into his stomach, causing him to splutter and spit out more blood. I stop as I see the blood splatter my jeans, and I slowly—very slowly—raise my head to look at him. I see him gulp as an evil smirk finds my lips.

"You really shouldn't have done that. I just washed these," I say as I kick him so hard in the shin that I hear a cracking sound. He howls in pain and then I grab his hair and pull his head back, getting right in his face, my teeth gritted together as I say, "And don't call her a bitch again."

"Why not?" he rasps. "Don't you hate her?"

"And what the fuck has it got to do with you?" I growl.

"Why else would you want us to kidnap her and take her to that creepy as fuck house?" he questions.

"I'm the only one here that asks questions," I tell him, letting go of his hair and standing back a little. I don't need to answer to these two lowlifes, and I'd rather ignore the fact that I feel bad about Zoey getting hurt, because I don't know what the fuck to do with that when it was my whole aim to make her suffer. "And with that being said, let's start, shall we?" I continue, needing to focus my energy on anything other than my thoughts.

"Start what?" Clint asks as Peter sits in the chair beside him—also tied up like Clint—looking like he is about to shit his pants.

"Question time," I begin. "One or two?" I ask Clint, without expanding on my question any further.

"One or two what?" he says.

"Just pick a number, asshole."

"Fine," he says, defeated. "One."

"Hands or feet?"

"I don't fucking know," he says. "What kinds of questions are these?"

"Ones that you will have the answers to very soon," I say, keeping my face deadpan. "Hands or feet?" I reiterate.

"Feet."

"Hammer or knife?"

"Hammer."

"Good. My favourite," I say as I walk over to the side and pull a hammer out of the cupboard before I walk back over to him, rip one of his shoes off his feet and then smash the hammer down. The scream that leaves him pierces my ears, but the sound of his bones cracking is worth listening to him scream like a fucking girl.

Peter looks like he's about to puke, and I'm hoping that this little display will make him realise how badly they screwed up.

I wait for the screaming to die down before I say, "Bet you're glad you only picked one and not two." The sarcasm drips from my voice, and tears fall from his eyes.

"Why are you doing this, Jax?" Clint asks.

"Because I can, and because you fucking hurt her," I rage, feeling my blood boiling all over again.

"And why the hell do you care? Surely you want her to pay for what she did?" he says, bold as brass, whilst Peter audibly gulps.

"How do you mean?" I reply in a low and deadly voice.

"No point acting all coy now, Jax. I know she is the reason your brother is dead."

"How do you know that?" I question before I can stop myself. We kept everything under wraps as much as possible, so for this weasel to know, it can only mean one thing…

"It seems you've got a leak in your group," Clint says as he smiles, blood coating his teeth. "She killed your brother and then she left, and you're so fucking past knowing what to do it's laughable—"

I snap. I unleash every ounce of fury on the bastard, and I pound my fists into his face, knocking him backwards, the chair crashing to the floor, him still tied to it as I pummel his face to pulp.

I keep going, needing to let out more aggression. I feel a hand rest on my shoulder, and I whirl around, ready to make mincemeat of whoever it is touching me, until I see that it's Kev, with Shorty stood just behind him.

I stop, my fist mid-air, and I stare at them with wide and wild eyes.

I look from their stoic faces to the blood coating my skin, and then my eyes move to the mess on the floor. The unrecognisable mess that was Clint.

I replay his words over in my mind. *"She killed your brother… She left… She killed your brother…"*

She killed my brother.

"Jax, let us take it from here," Kev says as he tentatively

looks at me. I nod at him and walk towards the exit, hearing him instructing Shorty to do… something. I can hear him speaking but the words aren't registering. I'm on autopilot as I go outside and get back on my bike, revving the engine before pulling away and heading back to the bar.

She killed my brother.

And for that alone, she's the one that needs to pay.

## Chapter Twenty

### Zoey

I stare at the ceiling, counting numbers in my head to pass the time.

Fifteen thousand and seventy-two.

Fifteen thousand and seventy-three.

It's my shitty effort at trying to decipher how much time has passed since Jax walked out of here, but of course, I've lost count several times and started all over again about twenty.

I've cried so many tears since Jax walked out of here, and I know I deserve this. I deserve to suffer for the pain that I've caused.

I've always been impatient and kept on and on until I've gotten my own way—my brother will attest to that. But I know that I changed everything when I decided to try and take down Jessica and Lucas. I did it with only good intentions to save Nate from having to hurt Jessica himself, but I should have waited. I was in way over my head and innocent people died from my mistake.

But they're not still here suffering—Jax is. There doesn't seem to be any end to his grief, not from what I can see, so if he feels he needs to do this to help ease his pain, then I'll let him. If he feels he needs to hurt me to make himself better, then he can do it. Because as much as I've tried to fight for the last five years, I'm just so fucking tired of it all.

I'm tired of whining.

I'm tired of feeling what I feel.

And I'm exhausted from trying to push away whatever the hell it is I feel for Jax Jones. Because I don't hate him, not even a little bit.

I get up off the bed and start to pace the room, because every now and again I need to stretch my legs—even if it is only a few steps one way and a few back again. I'm surprised I have any energy left to walk as I haven't eaten since Jax brought me a crappy sandwich yesterday… or was it today? I have no fucking idea because I've lost track of all time. It could have been today, but with nothing to break the monotony, I have no real clue.

I pace some more, just wanting the outcome of whatever the hell this is to be over and done with. And I guess I might get my answer as the door flies open, hitting the wall with a loud bang. My head shoots up to see Jax stood in the doorway, looking all kinds of pissed off. His eyes are dark, his expression grim, and his shoulders are heaving, like he's just done a full-on gym session that has kicked his ass.

Seconds pass by, he does nothing. He just stares at me, his eyes fixed on mine. I'm unable to look away from him because he commands the room. Even in this moment, I can appreciate that he is a formidable man with rugged good looks and a scowl that could melt your fucking underwear.

"Jax," I say quietly, and it's like my voice was the switch for him as he charges towards me. I don't have time to do anything except brace myself for the impact as his chest pushes into mine and he walks me back towards the wall, his hand going around my throat, his other pinning my wrists above my head. He pins my hips in place with his, and even as I feel his fingers start to apply pressure around my throat, all I want him to do is kiss me, taste me, feel me. I can't even hate him in this moment as I feel my airways closing a little more with each second that passes. I don't hate him—I never have. There's always been something about him that intrigues me and makes me want to know more, but my time is up. This has been a long time coming. He's been waiting to find me, to make me pay, and now he'll get his wish.

There would be no point trying to fight even if I wanted to. I'm weak, pathetic, and no longer the woman that I once was.

"You fucking killed him," he growls, and I feel the first tear fall down my cheek. "And you've made me into the fucking monster that I am today."

"Jax, please," I say as panic surges through me.

"You made me do it. You made me fucking do it," he rages.

"Made you do what?" I manage to choke out as I feel his fingers grip me harder.

"You really believe that I found you by accident when they rammed your car off the road?" he says, his eyes wild.

"You? It was you? You sent that guy to kidnap me?" I choke past the tears that are clogging my throat.

"Of course it was fucking me," he says, his face inches

from mine, his eyes piercing me like a dagger to the heart. "But once again you fucked everything up."

I feel the last little bit of fight leave my body.

I feel my mind shutting down.

I broke him, and now he's broken me.

And I say the only thing I can, because in this moment, I know it's all over. "I'm… so… sorry," I manage to rasp as his fingers clamp hard enough to cut off the air supply. My eyes are still locked to his as my tears blur his face, and then I close my eyes and hope that this doesn't take long.

I feel my arms go limp, my legs wanting to give way, my eyes closing as tiredness creeps up on me. I don't even feel pain because I've been riddled with it for so long that I don't feel much else anyway.

I wish I could have said goodbye to my brother, to Kat, to my beautiful Gracie… I wish I could have met the baby just once, but it wasn't meant to be—not for me anyway.

Tears continue to slide down my cheeks, even with my eyes being closed. My mind becomes hazy, a fog obscuring the memories.

Any second now and I'll finally be at peace.

# Chapter Twenty-One

## Jax

My hands find her neck as I push her back against the wall, my other hand locking her wrists together above her head.

Rage is fuelling me.

I need to end this.

I need to move the fuck on and stop letting grief rule my every waking moment.

This is how I start to live again. Destroying Zoey Knowles.

I've never put my hands on a woman like this before, but she is the exception to the rule. I can't explain how fucking crazy I feel right now. I hate her. I really fucking hate her.

But as I watch her body start to weaken, her eyes closing and silent tears falling down her cheeks, I have to question why this feels painful. Why this feels like I've hit rock fucking bottom and there is no way up. Why the thought of losing her makes my heart pound violently against my ribcage.

And then it hits me.

I don't hate her at all.

And that is what I am struggling with more than anything.

I actually fucking feel something for her.

The realisation has me moving my hand from her throat quicker than I put it there. I gently bring her wrists down from above her head and then my arms are sliding around her and I'm lifting her limp body into my arms as I go and lay her on the bed.

Fuck.

Please still be breathing. Please. Please. Fucking please.

I feel her pulse and breathe a sigh of relief. And then I lose it, but not in the angry way I just did—instead, I do the one thing I haven't done before and I let go of all of the sadness inside of me as I bury my face in her neck and apologise over and over again.

"I'm so fucking sorry," I say as I feel my walls crumble, my barrier being smashed to smithereens. I've spent so long in the dark, trapped in a hatred of my own doing. Yes, Zoey is the reason that Jason was there on that fateful day, but she didn't force him to go. She didn't hold a fucking gun to his head and march him there against his own freewill. He went because he wanted to. He made the decision to go without me.

*Without me.*

And that's the crux of the problem.

I wasn't there.

I couldn't help.

I didn't get the chance to try and do anything because I was dealing with some other shit that I can't even remember now—clearly it wasn't important.

I feel guilt for being absent.

I feel pain for not being by my brother's side.

I thought vengeance was the answer but look at what I've just done. I nearly killed her. I nearly took Zoey's life, and for what?

I can't even answer that question because there isn't a good enough answer.

As my guilt over hurting her consumes me, I fail to notice anything else until I feel a hand touch the back of my head. I pull my face from the crook of her neck and move back, seeing that her eyes are open.

"Zoey," I whisper as I bring my forehead to hers and rest it there. Her fingers softly stroke through my hair as I tell her that I'm sorry.

"It's okay," she whispers back. "I understand."

"No," I say as I pull my head back slightly and lock my eyes with hers. "No, you don't." It's the last thing I say before I feel that pull between us bringing my mouth to hers in a soft and gentle kiss.

I half expect her to push me off, kick me in the balls and scream at me to get off of her—and no one could blame her at this point—but she doesn't. Instead, her fingers tangle in my hair and her lips move against mine.

I'm careful not to put my weight on her as I climb over her body, placing my elbows either side of her head, propping myself up, our lips never losing contact.

Her hands move to my shoulders, her nails lightly raking down my arms.

And when we finally come up for air, she only asks one thing of me.

"Hold me, Jax."

And I do. I lie behind her, holding her close, her back to

my chest, my arm around her waist with her hand resting on top of mine, and we stay that way until the pull of sleep is too much to ignore.

And despite what transpired not so long ago, I'm pretty sure that this will be the best sleep I've had in a long time.

## Chapter Twenty-Two

### Jax

"Huh hum."

I hear the noise before I open my eyes, to see Kev stood in the doorway of the room I've been keeping Zoey in, and he has a big fucking smirk on his face.

"Made up, did we?" he says, all smug and shit.

"Fuck off," I grunt at him as I quickly check to make sure Zoey is asleep. She appears to be, so I slowly untangle myself from her, not wanting to wake her just yet. I walk around the bed and over to Kev, pulling the door closed behind me.

"What's the deal then, Jax?" Kev asks me seriously as I rake my hand through my hair.

"You mean you're not gonna grill me like a fucking chick?" I say, sarcasm edging into my voice.

"No need. I think it's pretty obvious that you no longer have plans to kill her," he comments.

"I don't?"

"No. And let's be honest, you never really did." Oh fucking hell, he has no idea how untrue that statement is, because I nearly did in fact kill her last night, until I regained my goddamn senses and had an epiphany or whatever the hell you want to call it.

"I'm going to take her back to my place for a couple of days," I tell him.

"You going off grid?"

"Just for forty-eight hours." I need to. I mean, I know this will take longer than forty-eight hours to fix, but hopefully it will be enough for now.

"And what about Cole? Because that Peter guy gave everything up that he knew the moment you left the room."

Cole.

Fuck.

"Which was?" I ask.

"That Cole has been working us the whole time, playing us for fools whilst he had designs to take Zoey and…"

"And what?" I question, my brow furrowed as Kev looks like he doesn't want to tell me the next part. "Kev, spit it out," I urge.

"Put her in the trafficking ring," he finishes, and I feel my blood boil.

"Motherfucker," I rage before I compose myself enough to say, "Cole is a snake and a traitor. There is no longer a place for him here."

"I figured, but what exactly do you want to do about it?" he questions, because usually I would be on top of this, and it would be a priority—one of the brothers going against us is not something I like to let linger, not to mention the fact that he's clearly tangled up in some nasty shit that can't be left for too long.

"Keep an eye on him. Get Gator to watch him from a distance." Gator is the newest member of the crew, but he's proven himself enough to have my trust to handle this. "And you and Shorty take care of things here. I take it you got rid of the bodies from last night?"

"Of course," he says as he scoffs, like I shouldn't even have bothered to ask. I mean, it was only right to get rid of them both because they knew too much—and add in the fact that I had beaten Clint to a bloody pulp, of course. "You know, Jax, our crew is getting smaller."

"I know." There's only the four of us now—me, Kev, Shorty and Gator. It's not enough. We need more, but it's hard to find the right people that fit.

"We'll manage. Go and sort your shit out and come back more like the old Jax," he says as he claps my shoulder before walking away.

The old Jax.

I haven't been him in a long time.

I mean, I was a miserable fucker before, but at least I lived. The last five years have all been about revenge, and there isn't much time to party when you're obsessed with finding someone.

With a sigh, I turn around and push the door back open to see Zoey sat on the bed, her back resting against the headboard and her arms hugging her knees. She looks so small and nothing like the devious woman I kept convincing myself she was. She looks tired, like she's had enough of all of the back and forth, and when my eyes see the marks around her neck, I feel a pang in my chest. I did that. I put those marks there. If I could take it back, I would, but I can't, and this is just another shitty decision that I have to live with.

I make my way over to her and she lifts her eyes to look at me. Eyes that used to sparkle but are now dull and lifeless.

"Morning," I say quietly as I sit down on the edge of the bed, shame filling me as I try not to look at her neck.

"Morning," she croaks out. I realise she probably needs a drink, but I also want to get out of here and have some breathing space back at my place.

"We're going back to my place today," I tell her. "Just for a couple of days."

"Okay."

Okay? That's it? No argument? No strop? No 'fuck off, Jax'?

"I guess we'll go now then," I tell her as I stand and hold my hand out to her. She hesitates for a second before placing her dainty hand in my palm. I clasp my fingers around hers as she gets off the bed and stands beside me. It's almost like last night never happened, and like I didn't admit that I planned to have her kidnapped—almost, because my head is a mindfuck of emotions.

Wordlessly, I lead her from the room and up the stairs, choosing to go out the back entrance, because I don't want her to have to walk through the front, even if it is just Kev in there.

I push the back door and make a beeline for my bike, which is just along the side of the building. When we get there, I reach for my helmet and then turn to Zoey. I lift the helmet above her head, but she steps back.

"What are you doing?" she asks.

"Putting my helmet on you."

"Why?"

"Just put it on," I answer, as if it's ridiculous that she's even asking me why in the first place.

"But what will you wear?" she says as her eyes dart to the bike, scanning it for another helmet.

"I'll be fine without one. And before you try to argue, it's not up for debate," I say with a smirk as I see a little flicker of defiance in her eyes. So it's still in there then? Good. I want that defiance to try to knock me on my ass. God knows I deserve it—although I won't be admitting that out loud.

I lift my arms and place the helmet over her head, doing it up tight enough that it doesn't fall off before turning to get on my bike. I start the engine and turn my head towards Zoey.

"Get on," I instruct, my eyes indicating that I expect her to sit behind me and hold on.

Her eyes are pinned to mine as I wait for her to get on the fucking bike so we can get out of here, but she slowly moves her arms and folds them over her chest, her foot tapping on the floor, making me smirk.

There's the fire.

It's still in there despite everything that's happened over the last couple of days—I just need to keep luring it out of her, one day at a time.

Speaking to her right now would do nothing, so I simply kick the bike stand out and then swing my leg over before I stalk towards her. Stopping in front of her, I say nothing, and then I lift her into my arms and carry her, because one way or another, she is getting on this bike.

"Put me down, Jax," she says, albeit a little muffled behind the helmet.

I ignore her and cock my leg over the bike, with her still in my arms.

"You gonna be a good girl and turn around so we can get the hell out of here?" I say.

"Good girl? Oh my God," she says with an eye roll.

"Turn around and sit the fuck down," I grit out, fully aware that the longer we're out here in the open, the more likely we are to be spotted by unwanted eyes—namely her brother and Ronan, because I know they are still hunting her down.

I see the challenge spark to life in her eyes, and maybe it's because we're out of that crappy room or maybe it's because of what happened last night, who fucking knows, but whatever it is, I want more.

She wriggles in my arms again and manoeuvres herself until she's sat so she's facing me, and then she lifts her legs and wraps them around my waist.

"I'm ready," she says as she grinds herself against my crotch, and fuck if I don't want to take her right here, right now. Bike sex. Interesting. I'll add it to my to-do list at some point, but for the moment, we need to get out of here and to the confines of my place.

I kick the bike stand back into place and rev the engine.

"Hold on tight, pretty girl." It's the only warning I give her before we're moving. I pick up speed quickly and her arms slide around the back of my neck. How the fuck I concentrate on the road is beyond me, but I seem to be managing okay as we fly along, twisting and turning. I try to block out thoughts of her pussy rubbing my dick through our clothes. I try to think about anything other than my mouth being on her, tasting her, devouring her. I try to expel all images of my dick pounding into her as her cries ring out with pleasure, but it's no use. Zoey Knowles is on a whole other level, and the fact that she can piss me off and make me want her in equal measure is nothing short of a miracle.

I weave around the few cars on the road, and this journey feels like the longest fucking bike ride in history. I clench my jaw, willing my dick to stop getting excited because I am supposed to fucking hate this woman. Thing is, it's all changed. The playing field is not what it once was—last night alone opened my eyes to that. I could have killed her. I could have watched her take her last breath, and I very nearly did, but I couldn't. The pain was far worse as I came to my senses and really looked at her.

Am I ready to forgive what happened though?

Only time will tell.

I see the turning to my place and I veer right, cutting in front of a car, hearing them beeping the horn as I rumble down the track. I slow it down a little as the house approaches, and then I pull to a stop by the front door.

Zoey is still holding onto me as I turn the engine off and kick the bike stand out before standing, lifting her with me. Her legs stay wrapped around me as I walk us to the front door. I unlock it and pull it open, stepping inside and shutting the door behind me.

Only then does she pull her head back, take the helmet off, and pin with me with her eyes.

"That was fucking exciting," she says, and I can hear something akin to joy in her voice.

I can't help but smirk as I take the helmet from her and place it on the table by the door before making my way through the house, stopping at the room she will use for the next couple of days.

"You'll be staying in here," I say as she lets her legs slide down until she's supporting herself and unwrapping her arms from around my neck.

"What, no basement with a lockable door?" she sasses.

"If I thought that you'd run then we would still be in that shitty room back at the bar," I tell her.

"And what makes you think I won't run?" she asks as I pin her with my gaze.

"You won't." I know she won't. She's still harbouring a shit load of guilt for her part in my brother's death, she wants forgiveness too much to try and leave. The fact that she was going to let me kill her told me that without any need for the words to come from her mouth.

"Pretty sure of yourself," she says as she turns and starts looking around the bedroom.

"If you can't bet on yourself in this life then it's just fucking pointless."

She stops and turns to look at me. "Huh. I never thought of it like that."

"Really? You brother is a crime lord and yet he never told you to own every decision and back yourself one hundred percent?" I find that hard to believe.

"*Was* a crime lord. And he taught me well," she says defensively.

"Sure he did." I've not really got anything against Nate, I just like pushing her buttons.

"Don't you stand there and try to judge my family," she fumes, her hands on her hips as she stares daggers at me. "You don't know shit about what we've been through, or what my brother has done for me."

"Fair point. Must be nice to still have a brother around."

Her face falls, and I know it was a low fucking blow, but I can't help it. It's like a reflex. She mentions something, I try to find a way to bring it back to Jason.

"You can't keep doing this, Jax. You can't keep fucking with me like this. I've apologised, I carry the guilt, I know you'll never fully forgive me for what happened, but for fuck's sake, just stop."

"I can't stop," I tell her, my voice low.

"You can."

"Zoey, it's been ingrained in me for so fucking long to hate you—"

"Yeah, I got the memo last night when you nearly fucking killed me," she says loudly, and then silence deafens the room as we stare at one another. I finally let my eyes wander to the marks around her neck once again, and I feel a rage inside of me that I need to expel. I'm fucking angry that I went that far, even if it had been my intention for years.

"Help yourself to anything you want," I say as I turn my back on her and she leaves me with her parting words.

"Yeah, because this is my new cage. Forever doomed to be a fucking prisoner."

## Chapter Twenty-Three

### Zoey

*"Forever doomed to be a fucking prisoner."*

It's what my life has been.

Born into the underworld. Sister to a crime lord. Ran away to the confines of an island. Traded the island for another type of enclosure all together.

I have never known any different.

All these powerful men that want to be the top fucking dog and control everything around them—I don't want it.

Granted, the protection of my family and their name alone has been helpful over the years, but if we were never in the underworld in the first place then I would have experienced a normal life and not one where there is a security detail lurking around the corner. And okay, I've dodged them many times and managed to do some things without them knowing, but the reality of my life is that nothing stays buried and I'll always be looking over my shoulder.

I'm starting to think that I should have just stayed away and lived with my pain. I shouldn't have come back because it's just made everything worse.

Not to mention that Nate is going to be doing his fucking nut, and God knows who he's killed to try and find me. He may have been on an island for five years, but he's trained to kill, and kill he will.

I sigh as I make my way to the ensuite shower in my room. I haven't seen Jax since he walked away earlier. I haven't even tried to go and look for him, because whatever happens always ends up in snarky comments and more anger—or something sexual. I should be scared after what he did, after what he admitted, but for some reason, I'm not. I even understand his actions… maybe I really am more fucked in the head than I ever realised?

I'm dying to phone Nate and tell him where I am, but I can't see a phone anywhere—that is the one thing I have looked for. But even if I found one, would I really phone him and get Jax in a world of shit? I mean, Jax knows that hiding me away isn't a smart idea, but if I were to find a phone and call Nate and tell him where I am, Jax would be dead within seconds of him arriving here. I don't think I can do that. Despite everything, I don't want to see Jax dead.

I shake my head and turn the shower on, stripping out of my clothes and throwing them on the floor before stepping under the hot water.

There is shampoo and body wash in here already, so I lather up my hands and start to wash away the last few days. The coconut smell of the shampoo and body wash engulfs me, and I close my eyes as I relish in the feeling of being clean.

I wash my hair and lather my body in suds again and again. It feels good. And what would feel even better is if I could just get the thought of Jax out of my mind. His body, his face, the way he exudes himself… it's all fucking good, and I wish that it wasn't.

I let my mind wander to places it shouldn't. His mouth, his tongue, his dick… and I slide my hand down my body until it reaches my pussy. I circle my finger on my clit as I picture him tasting me, eating me, taking me.

I turn and lean my back against the wall, and using my free hand, I pinch my nipple, moaning quietly from the sensations flowing through me.

I may have been through hell the last couple of days, but I'm still a woman with needs, and I need to find a release right now.

I get lost in my own head, blocking out reality and living in my imagination where Jax is knelt before me and his tongue replaces my finger. He grabs my thighs and digs his fingers in, holding me in place as he eats me like I'm his last meal. I imagine my fingers gripping his hair, my leg hooking over his shoulder, his fingers finding my opening and thrusting inside as he takes me higher and higher.

I imagine him groaning as I scream my release. I imagine him pinning me against the wall as his dick pounds inside of me. I imagine my nails scratching his skin, leaving marks as I claim him for my own.

My breathing is heavy as I open my eyes, and then I freeze.

Jax.

Stood in the doorway.

Watching me.

Fuck.

His eyes are trained on my pussy before they travel up my body and lock with mine.

And then something comes over me as I bite my bottom

lip and open my legs a little wider. I am aware that I should be nothing but pissed at him, and don't get me wrong, I could fucking wring his neck for holding me hostage, but in this moment, I struggle to muster any anger. And instead of anger, all I feel is this feral need to have his hands on me. I clearly have issues as I start to move my finger again slowly, and I watch as he watches me getting off. His eyes are blazing as I arch my back and run my other hand over my breasts.

He shouldn't be in here, in my personal space, but then I remember I don't have any personal space and it's actually hot as fuck having him watch me.

I move my hand from my breasts down to my pussy, and I push my legs wider as I open myself up more, so that he can see every fucking thing. And then I close my eyes again, because I need this. I need this release. I need this moment.

I feel myself building once again, the image of him standing in the doorway fresh in my mind and like my own little slice of paradise.

I like paradise—it's calm, peaceful, and oh-so-fucking hot.

But my imaginary paradise is quickly brought to reality as I feel his lips around my finger. I open my eyes as I think that I am still imagining things, but I'm not. Jax is knelt in front of me, his mouth on my clit as my finger moves in circles. His hands move to my thighs, much like my thoughts earlier, as he eats me. And I don't stop him as I look down, needing more.

His tongue moves with my finger, circling, and then he's ripping my hand away and gripping my wrist as he sucks my clit, hard.

I move my leg over his shoulder, and then he moves my other one, so I am completely at his mercy and being held up by him.

And then I scream as he grabs my ass and squeezes, and I orgasm.

I rock against him, his stubble feeling rough but good.

He takes everything from me before manoeuvring me so I'm sliding down the bathroom tiles until my ass hits the floor of the walk-in shower. It's big enough for me to lie down, and he climbs on top of me, his dick at my opening before he pushes inside of me.

He thrusts relentlessly, making me moan his name again and again. And then his lips find mine and we kiss like it's the last time we will ever be able to do so.

It's like we're two animals, biting, clawing.

The water rains down us, and he fucks me faster, harder, until my body starts to shake from the way he's hitting me so fucking deep.

I link my hands around his neck as he lifts me up so I'm in his lap, and then he's holding onto my thighs as I take a turn to fuck him hard and fast. His teeth find my nipple and he bites, but only enough to cause a little pain and a whole lot of pleasure. He then moves to the other one and does the same thing as I dig my nails in his shoulders and grind my hips.

This man makes me crazy. He makes me question my sanity, because essentially, I'm fucking the enemy.

And not one part of me gives a fuck about that as I scream out his name, my body shuddering on top of his, my pussy clenching around his dick as he roars with his release. I ride him until we're both spent, and then I kiss him slowly, savouring every second, because I know that this connection will be broken any minute now.

And when that moment comes, I'm left alone on the shower floor with tears falling down my cheeks and the water continuing to rain down on me.

## Chapter Twenty-Four

### Ronan

"Where the fuck is she?" Nate roars, and I fear that he may just lose complete control if we don't find Zoey soon.

It's been four days since that night at Purity.

Four days since she disappeared, and the longer she's missing, the worse the outcome will be.

"Why can't we trace her?"

"Because whoever took her knew what they were doing and made sure there was no trace to be found," I tell him. Neither of us have slept much, both surviving on strong coffee and hopes that are quickly fading.

"I will fucking annihilate whoever did this," he fumes, and I have no doubt that he will. Let's face it, he didn't become a ruthless leader for no reason.

"For fuck's sake, Nate, calm down," Kat says from her seat in the corner of the office.

"Kat, don't start with me," Nate warns, but she just smirks at him.

"I get that you're pissed but don't speak to me like that, ever," Kat replies, and Nate's eyes narrow on her.

"My sister is missing, and you want me to calm down?" he rages.

"Yes, because Zoey isn't fucking stupid," Kat answers back. "You taught her what to do, she knows how to handle herself, so stop thinking that she can't."

"Ronan, give us the room," Nate says, and I stand up, quite happy to get the hell out of here. I've known Kat and Nate a long time and they are either about to have an epic row or an epic fuck, and I don't need to be here for either.

I close the door behind me and make my way downstairs to pour yet another fucking vat of coffee.

"Ronan, we think we have a trace," one of the security team says as they walk in the kitchen, taking my attention away from the coffee.

"Where?"

"Highnam woods."

"Fuck." Highnam woods is where you go to cover up shit you don't want found. But hang on… "We've searched there already."

"Well, we think we missed some ripped fabric that got buried beneath dirt."

"*We* think?" I say incredulously. Fuck me, this is not good enough. "You mean, *you* think you missed something."

"Yes, boss." He doesn't even try and deny it because he's been on this for four days and should have found it the first time, which was day one of her being missing.

"I'll get Nate. Wait out front," I instruct before taking the stairs two at a time and racing down the hallway to the office. I don't even risk opening the door and instead I just bang on it and say, "Wrap it up, we gotta move out."

---

"Well?" Kat says when we walk back through the front door.

I walk straight past her and head for the kitchen. I don't mean to be rude, but I'm pissed.

"Dead end," I hear Nate say from behind me.

I don't hear anymore as I walk through the kitchen and make my way across the expanse of garden until I'm punching in the code for the building that sits on the edge of the property.

I flip the light switch as I enter and move to get some boxing gloves, putting them on so I can pound the shit out of something.

I don't even care that I'm in a goddamn suit as I pummel the bag in front of me, and it may seem strange that I'm getting so worked up, but Zoey is family to me, just like Nate is, and it kills me that we don't have a lead.

We always have a lead. Always. But not this time.

I don't know how long I'm in here for before I hear the door open, and I drop my arms and stretch out my neck as I see Kat walk in.

"Thought you might want a drink," she says as she holds out a bottle of whiskey. I laugh at the gesture because only Kat would bring alcohol when what I should probably have is water. I take the bottle and swig. The burn of the whiskey hits the back of my throat and I take another gulp. I could literally finish this whole fucking bottle right now.

"I get that you wanna find her, Ronan, but you and Nate running yourselves into the ground isn't the way to go about it," Kat says, and I pause with the bottle held to my lips.

"It is, and we won't stop until we find her," I say.

"I know that, but right now you're both too invested to think clearly. You need to take a break and really fucking think about things," she says, and if she weren't Nate's wife, I'd probably tell her she doesn't know shit. But she does. She knows how Nate works, and by extension, me.

"I can't take a break, Kat, you know that."

"Then you're rendered useless. And I've said exactly the same thing to Nate too, before you start to get ideas about favouritism." Her sarcasm has me shaking my head and smiling. Fuck I've missed these guys. It's been a lonely old road all by myself and I'm going to hate seeing them leave all over again. "You need to start thinking outside the box a little bit," she continues, and I frown.

Outside the box.

Outside the box.

Seconds tick by and turn into minutes as my mind races for an answer, and then, like a lightbulb going off in my head, my mind casts back to not so long ago, when I was at the Yates' house and Jax and Kev found me waiting for them.

*"What I want is something you won't ever give."* Jax's words. Something I won't ever give—Zoey being very fucking high on that list.

"Mother of fuck… you're a genius," I say.

"Tell me something I don't know," she replies with a laugh.

"I gotta go." And without waiting any longer, I hand her back the bottle of whiskey and make a run back to the house.

There are only a few places we haven't searched, J's bar

and the bikers houses, because I was confident that there would be no need to, but it's an oversight on my part, and I plan to rectify that right fucking now.

# Chapter Twenty-Five

## Jax

I sip the cold beer and stare out at the dark sky.

I left her in the shower after we fucked, on the floor and all alone.

I'm a bastard.

I need to stop this fucking merry-go-round that we seem to be on. It's no good to either of us.

So much history. So much shit. I'm tired of it all.

I want her. I mean, I really fucking want her, more than I've ever wanted anyone before.

The way we talk, the way we fuck—it's like she was made for me.

If only I'd admitted that I wanted her way back when, then none of this mess would have happened because she would have been mine and she would have phoned me on that day when she tried to take on the world herself. She wouldn't have phoned Jason and I would have made sure she hadn't gone in all guns blazing because she would have been mine to protect. To love. To fucking worship.

I'm not one for falling in love, but for her… fuck… I'm already falling. I know I am, and I hate myself for it.

I hear her before I see her, her feet padding across the patio behind me.

"Here," she says as a beer bottle is thrust in front of me. "I thought you could use another one, seeing as you've been out here for a while."

I finish the bottle already in my hand and place it on the floor beside me, taking the new bottle from her. "Thanks."

She takes the seat next to me, and I see she has a beer of her own.

Why does she even want to be near me at this point? I've done nothing but blow hot and cold with her since she came back.

"It's a nice night," she comments as she looks across the backyard. I notice she's wearing one of my shirts, a pair of my boxers and nothing else, because there are no other clothes for her here, and the ones she wore here are on the airer in the porch from where she obviously washed them earlier.

"Nice clothes," I remark with an edge of amusement.

She laughs lightly and the sound makes something inside of me crack.

"Jax, I know you've struggled since I've been back, and I came here to make peace with what happened, but clearly that's not working… so when you're ready to let me leave, I'm going to go far away again. And not because I'm running, but because I know that having me here is hurting you, and I need that to stop," she says quietly, shocking the hell out of me. "I can't be the cause of anymore of your pain, and I'm okay with not healing my own because I don't deserve forgiveness for what I did. I get that now. I was naïve to think it could ever be given.

"And I am truly sorry for all of the hurt that I've brought to your life. I never wanted to hurt you, Jax," she says, keeping her head straight, her eyes fixed ahead as I stare at her side profile.

I look at her nose, her lips, her hair falling down her back, her eyelids blinking a little more rapidly than they were when she first sat down.

Will her leaving help me?

Will it squash the fucking despair I feel?

"You know, I think about how different things could have been—how I should have been less selfish and more cautious. I really thought I had that plan all figured out, and I was proud of myself, you know? I was proud that I was going to save my brother from something that would have killed a part of him. I was proud to do that, to have my moment where I showed everyone that I could take care of shit myself. And yes, I saved my brother from inflicting pain on a woman—something he had never done before. But in saving my brother, I cost you yours." She pauses as she finally turns her head to look at me.

"And I know that if it had been the other way around, if my brother was dead because of you… I get it. I get why you hate me, but I wish that you didn't."

I feel a lump form in my throat—what the fuck is this? I don't get emotional like this, but her words, her grief which is plain as day on her face… it's painful to witness.

She looks at me with hopelessness, because she thinks that I despise her… but I don't.

I fucking don't.

And this is the moment where I decide to either own my life or keep my head buried in the sand.

Do I betray my brother?

Would he see it as a betrayal?

There is no fucking handbook for this. There are no rules. We're on our own playing field, trying to figure it all out as we go along.

The words get stuck in my throat as I open my mouth to speak, and her eyes close as she gently nods her head.

"I understand," she whispers, and then she stands up and starts to walk away.

Fuck.

I feel something akin to panic as my eyes watch her walking back to the house, and it isn't until her hand rests on the doorknob that I finally find my voice.

"You're wrong," I say loudly, and she freezes but keeps her back to me. "You're so far from the truth of what's going on here."

Silence.

I guess she said her piece and now I have to say mine.

"I have put so much energy into hating you over the years. It's taken up so much of my head space—"

"I get it," she says quietly, but I hear her. I can't speak to her like this, with her not even facing me.

"Look at me," I tell her as I take a few steps forward. She shakes her head, so I try again. "Zoey, look at me."

The air is still, no noise to be heard apart from the soft sigh she releases before she turns around, her head hanging down.

"Look. At. Me," I repeat, more firmly.

Her head slowly lifts, and her tearful eyes connect with mine.

I take a moment.

I allow myself the time to truly appreciate that she is stood before me. She may look defeated but she's a fighter. She's my fighter. Mine.

"I don't hate you, pretty girl." I take another step towards her.

"Don't say things you don't mean, Jax."

I keep moving forwards, advancing on my prey.

"You of all people should know that I don't." I come to a stop in front of her, and my hands cup her face as I say, "I shouldn't want you, but I do. I want you so fucking bad…" And then my lips are softly touching hers. This isn't rushed, this isn't hurried. I am a man of actions more than words, and although my actions may have been all over the goddamn place recently, I'm hoping this action conveys that I do feel something. Something more than just wanting this woman.

I entwine my tongue with hers.

I feel her tears on my cheeks, and I give her everything I possibly can at this moment in time.

I give her me.

# Chapter Twenty-Six

## Zoey

He's kissing me like I'm about to break. Like I'm fragile glass that could shatter at any moment.

I guess he isn't far wrong, because I am the definition of someone who is balancing on a knife's edge.

*"I don't hate you, pretty girl."*

Those words.

I've wanted to hear them for so fucking long—to know that he truly meant them. No games. No bullshit.

My tongue meets his and everything feels right with the world.

And when he lifts me into his arms and carries me back inside, walking me to his bedroom and placing me gently on the bed, his body covering mine, I feel like I've truly come home.

There has always been something about Jax.

I've always found him attractive, appealing, but he was

always so closed off. He's been that way for so long, and I know that this moment is something he won't have taken lightly.

We've been battling whatever this is since I came back.

The tension, the emotions, the drama, the indecision, it's all been leading to this moment.

I should want to see him suffer for nearly killing me.

I should want him to feel pain for inflicting weeks of hot and cold on me.

But I don't.

None of that matters right now. Some would say that I'm being too soft, too lenient, considering his actions, but they don't know our history, they don't know our battle, and I could make him grovel for the next ten years, but all that would do is keep dragging up the past, and I am so fucking done with the past.

We have a lot of shit to work through, I know that, but we can deal with that tomorrow, or the next day, or the day after that.

The only thing that matters now is Jax unbuttoning the shirt I'm wearing, his lips leaving mine and trailing down my neck, over my breasts, down my stomach, along my thighs and then hitting my sweet spot. He's gentle, soft, unlike the other times before.

His fingers caress my thighs, and my orgasm builds slowly. And when I'm close to finding my release, I am about to tell him to stop when he seems to read my mind and moves up my body, trailing kisses all the way until he reaches my mouth.

An understanding passes between us, one we won't argue about.

I want him to be inside me when I come this time, and he seems to already know that.

He pushes off me and stands so he can take off his T-shirt and jeans to reveal that he is actually commando underneath.

He climbs back on top of me and places his forehead against mine as he enters me. I open my legs wider and wrap them around his waist. He starts to move in and out of me slowly, savouring every stroke.

I move my hands to the tops of his arms, letting my fingers feel his biceps. My orgasm starts to build again, and then he moves his hand down until his thumb is circling my clit in time with his tortuously delicious rhythm.

My walls clench around him and then he whispers, "Come for me, pretty girl."

He increases the pressure on my clit, and a few seconds later, I orgasm, feeling every inch of it from my head to my toes. My skin tingles, my eyes see stars, and my body trembles.

Jax follows and moans as I lift my head and place my lips on his. And even when we're spent, he stays on top of me, kissing me as if this has all been a dream and it's about to disappear any second now.

But this isn't a dream.

This is real.

It just took us a moment to get here, to figure it out.

I don't know how long our lips are locked together.

I don't know how long our second round of love making takes, because that's what this is. Love making. It's not fucking. It's more. So much more.

All I know is that after, Jax pulls the duvet over us, takes me in his arms and holds me against him as I fall asleep feeling content and satisfied, because this struggle between us is over. It's done. And even with issues still between us, this is the start of something neither of us expected—something new, something that will have ugly moments but will be beautiful at the end of it.

Jax Jones, always known as the untouchable brother, but maybe, just maybe, he is untouchable no more.

---

I wake up with Jax's arms wrapped around me and I can't help but allow a smile to grace my lips. My back is to his chest as I feel him shift behind me, his lips coming to my ear as he says in his deep voice, "Good morning, pretty girl." And then his tongue darts out and licks the shell of my ear before his lips find my neck.

I half expected to wake up and find him gone, going back to being cold again, but this… this is just fucking perfect. And I know that this feeling of bliss won't last much longer, so I'm going to enjoy every single second until the bubble I've found myself in is popped and reality works its way back in to try and fuck shit up all over again.

I arch my neck a little more, allowing him more access as I bring my hand up and place it behind his head, threading my fingers through his hair. I sigh with contentment before turning my head towards him so he can bring his lips to mine.

I moan into his mouth as his hand moves from my waist and trails to my pussy, his fingers trailing up and down before he's moving my leg, hooking it over his hip, leaving me completely exposed for his fingers to work their magic. And oh boy do they do just that as he pushes two fingers inside of me as his thumb continues to rub my clit until I cum on his hand. He swallows my moans as his tongue continues to caress mine, and when he removes his hand from my pussy, he breaks our lips apart and sucks his fingers. Didn't think that would be so hot, but fuck, it really is.

I turn around so my body is facing him, and then I taste myself on his lips before moving down his body until I get to his cock. His very hard cock.

I slowly put my mouth over him, moving up and down, swirling my tongue around the tip as I come back up before taking him all the way to the back of my throat as I go back down. Can't say I've ever really enjoyed giving a blow job before, but when his thighs clench and he groans as he releases in my mouth, I can honestly say that it makes me feel fucking horny.

His hands reach down and hook under my arms as he pulls me back up and then cages me beneath his body. He just stares at me, like he's trying to figure out something.

"You okay there?" I ask quietly.

"I'm very okay," he says as he dips his head and places a quick kiss on my lips before saying, "Coffee?"

Bloody hell, this is all so surreal. It's like I'm living in the twilight zone.

When I went to him last night in the garden, I never expected this to be how things turned out. Funny how life throws a curveball at you when you least expect it.

"Please."

He smiles and climbs off of me, getting off the bed and grabbing a pair of grey joggers from his closet. He pulls them on, and I move to the edge of the bed, suddenly feeling self-conscious as I wrap my arms around myself. I don't know why, it's not like it's the first time he's seeing me naked.

"You don't need to be shy around me, Zoey," he comments.

"I know, but this is just…"

"Different," he finishes.

"Yeah."

"I know, but don't ever hide from me," he says, his voice low and laced with some kind of… warning? Threat?

"Just so you know, Jax, you don't get to issue me with some shitty threat," I say, feeling my sass spark to life.

I bend down and pick up the shirt I was wearing last night, putting it on and feeling his eyes watching my every move.

"You think that was a threat?" he says incredulously. "Pretty girl, you have no idea."

"Then what the fuck was it? Because we've just had a beautiful moment and then you go and ruin it by telling me not to hide from you."

"Jesus Christ," he says with an eye roll. "That was not a threat. That was me telling you not to hide this body from me," he says as he reaches over and pulls the shirt open, exposing me to him. "That was me telling you that nothing can be hidden between us—not this body, not the way you feel, not now, not ever, because I am all fucking in."

"Oh."

He's all in.

All fucking in.

Well, damn.

"You mean, even with my tendency to think the worst and the way I can be a little dramatic at times, you're still all in?"

He chuckles as he pulls me to him. "Yes, Zoey. That is what I'm telling you."

"But we have so much to talk about…"

"And we will, but no matter what happens, I'm still all in, and I swear to you that I will do everything I can to make up for what I have done to you."

"But—" He cuts me off by dropping a kiss on my lips.

"The 'but' can wait until after we've had a coffee, or five."

I playfully punch his arm and he laughs. Jax Jones laughs, and it's a real laugh. One I could get used to hearing—and I hope I do.

I pull on a clean pair of his boxers and then link my fingers with his as he leads me from the bedroom to the kitchen. I take a seat at the table and button up my shirt as he fills the kettle and grabs a couple of mugs. He makes the drinks and then places my mug in front of me before sitting opposite.

"So, Jax, at the risk of ruining the mood, I have to know something…" I bite my lip as he looks at me intently. "What is this? What are we doing here?" My heart is racing in my chest at what his answer might be.

"We're drinking coffee."

"Ha-ha," I say sarcastically. Him cracking a joke is a good sign, but I want to try and be realistic about this. My hopes soared last night when he said he didn't hate me. They soared even higher when he made love to me. They went off the fucking charts when I woke up in his arms. But this is a complete one-eighty, and I need to protect my already fragile heart. "What I mean is, how have we gone from what we were to this? To sipping coffee and smiling instead of snarky comments or hate fuelled fucking."

"Hate fuelled fucking?" he says with an arch of his eyebrow.

"Well, yeah. That's what we did, right?" No. I never hated him.

He runs a hand over his face before putting both elbows on the table, leaning forward a little.

"I don't know if hate is the right word for it. Sure, I *thought* I hated you. I tried to convince myself that I did, but I don't think it was hate at all."

"Then what was it?"

"It was me hating myself for wanting you, because…"

"Because of Jason," I finish for him, mentioning the elephant in the room—his brother.

"Christ," he says as he sighs and gets up, going back to the kettle and clicking it on again, even though we've hardly touched our drinks. He turns and puts his hands on the worktop, his shoulders hunched and his head hanging down.

This needs to stop.

I get up and go over to him, putting my arms around his waist as I hug him from behind.

"He would want you to be happy, Jax." I place a kiss in the centre of his back which is still bare because he never put a T-shirt on.

"He always knew I wanted you," he says, nearly knocking me on my ass. I loosen my hold on him and he turns around, his eyes boring into mine.

"What?" I whisper.

"Yeah, he knew. He was my brother, he was the only person who really knew me, but I always told him that I had no interest because I knew he wanted you too."

I have no words. I didn't expect this to come out of his mouth.

"Jax…"

"I wish I hadn't been so fucking stubborn because this could have all been so different," he says as he moves a strand of hair away from my cheek.

"I'm sorry." It's all I can think to say.

"Me too."

I place my head on his chest and hug him tight. He rests his chin on top of my head and we stay like that until a knock on the front door has us breaking apart. He frowns as he lets go of me and makes his way to the front door. I stay rooted to the spot, thinking about what he just told me.

Jax always wanted me.

Dear God, my life is like a damn soap opera.

I hear muffled voices at the door and then there's an almighty bang that has me spinning around quickly. I hear footsteps pounding down the hallway and my instincts tell me that whatever is about to happen isn't good. I dart to the left, grabbing a knife out of the block on the worktop. Turning around, a guy with short dark hair comes into view, his dark eyes wide as he focuses on me.

I hold the knife in front of me, ready to go on the attack if needs be.

"Who the fuck are you?" I question, keeping my voice firm. Now is not the time to be scared. Now is the time to think logically and make the right choice.

"Zoey Knowles, well, well, well," he drawls, and the way he licks his lips makes my skin crawl.

"Who are you?" I repeat.

"There's no need to fear me. Come on, put the knife down and we'll just talk."

"Like hell we will."

"Feisty. I can see we're going to have some fun with you," he says, his eyes raking over my bare legs. There is no way that this guy is getting his hands on me.

"Well, at least tell me your name so I know who is trying to threaten me," I say.

"This ain't no threat, babe. I'm the real deal."

"Ugh. Cliché too. Wonderful. Did they leave the real boss at home and send the lacky in to do the dirty work?" I goad, and like a moth to a flame he takes the bait, charging for me, but I've already predicted his move as I duck down and kick my leg out, swiping him off his feet. He falls to the ground with a loud cry of anger, and I make my move, swiping the knife across his Achilles' heel—both of them—and his anger turns to cries of pain. He turns over, howling the place down, and then I hear more feet coming down the hallway. Fuck.

I make a quick exit out of the back door and charge for the fence at the back. I may not be dressed appropriately, but when your life is on the line, you'll haul ass so fucking quick that you won't even have time to think about clothes or injuries. Adrenaline is my fuel as I make it to the fence, but I'm not quick enough to scale it as I'm hauled back against a firm chest.

"Oh no you don't," I hear as my hand is smashed against the fence, the impact making me drop the knife.

"Get off of me, you asshole," I shout as I wriggle in his grip.

"Fuck's sake, get a gag on this bitch and get her tied up," he barks. My eyes zone in on the two guys walking towards us, both with masks over their faces, hiding their identity. Pussies.

I try as hard as I can to get free, but then I see one of the men raise his hand, and a blow to the head leaves me feeling groggy, my eyes closing as pain sears through me, and then everything goes dark as something is shoved over my head, encasing me in darkness.

# Chapter Twenty-Seven

## Jax

Fucking Cole.

The guys were meant to be watching him, so what the hell happened for him to show up on my doorstep with an entourage?

I groggily sit up and my hands fly to my head which is throbbing, but my body is moving despite the pain because I need to find Zoey.

"Zoey," I call out, wincing at the way my voice booms.

I can't hear a damn thing as I make my way through the house, hoping she's just hiding somewhere.

"Zoey, they've gone," I bark, but still nothing.

After searching the garden and every single room, I quickly come to the conclusion that Cole and the fuckers that were with him have taken her. Shit. The blood on the kitchen floor is making me feel even more panicked—something I don't feel too often, and I don't fucking like it one little bit.

I rush to the bedroom and pick my jeans up off the floor, pulling my phone out and quickly dialling Kev to see why no one was watching him.

The phone rings four times, and when he picks up, I don't give him a chance to speak as I shout down the phone, "Why the fuck did no one have eyes on him?" I won't need to explain because Cole was the only fucker anyone was supposed to have eyes on.

"Jax, we've had shit going on at the bar. Ronan and his men have been turning the place over," Kev tells me.

"What?" Oh jeez, this just gets worse.

"They're on their way to yours now. I was about to call you, they've just left, but they are convinced that you have Zoey."

"Shit," I say as I grab a T-shirt and march from the bedroom to the kitchen, quickly grabbing some painkillers and washing them down with some water.

"You need to get her out of there, man."

"She's already gone. Cole has her," I inform him. "Fucker stormed my place not so long ago, knocked me out, and then took her." Even saying the words causes a fucking pain inside of me. I failed her, again.

"We'll find them," he tells me before he's shouting out, "Shorty, get the fucking tracker up, we've got work to do."

I don't need to give him any instructions because he already knows what to do.

"I'll see you soon," I tell him and then hang up the phone. I need to get the fuck out of here before Ronan and co tear the place up. I don't have time to deal with their shitty interrogation. I'm going straight to a source who I know will work with me first before he decides to kill me—I'm going to see Nate.

"Nate," I say when the door opens and he stands there, his eyes narrowed on me.

"Jax."

"Can we talk?" A few beats of silence pass before I add, "About Zoey."

His jaw clenches and he steps aside for me to enter. Nate never scared me, and he fucking knows it. He may be able to intimidate most people, but not me. We've had minimal interaction over the years because he stayed on his turf and I stayed on mine, but now our worlds have collided, and all that really matters right now is finding Zoey.

"Follow me," he says once he's shut the front door. He leads me down the hallway and to a door on the left. We enter what is a large dining room and he walks around the table, sitting down and gesturing for me to sit opposite.

"I assume you know where my sister is," he says, not even bothering with any kind of small talk.

"Not exactly, but together we can find her a hell of a lot quicker than we could on our own."

"You better talk real fast," he says, an underlying threat in his tone.

"Before I do, just know that I care about your sister, and whatever happened before can be dealt with once she's safe."

"Fine," he grits out. "Start talking."

I tell him everything—well, almost everything. I omit the parts where I fucked his sister several times, because no brother wants to hear that. I also fail to mention that I nearly killed her because he doesn't need to focus on that right now, not when her life hangs in the balance. But I do tell him that she's been with me for the last few days and that I wiped any trace of anyone finding her because we had shit that needed to be dealt with. If Zoey chooses to tell him everything, then that's her call and I won't stop her. If I am to be punished for what I did to her, then so be it. I made those decisions and I have to own every single one, if it comes to that.

"So Cole has been working with the Yates' acquaintances?"

"It appears so. After I ousted him for six months, he obviously took it badly, despite already working against us."

"No shit. And you did that because he was Ronan's puppet behind the scenes." Not a question but a statement. "And how do you know that these guys with him were acquaintances of the Yates'?"

"The same way you know everything about someone when they're on your radar. I watched them for long enough to know who came and went."

Nate nods and then he's pulling a phone out of his pocket and barking orders down the line. My own phone rings and I look to see that an unknown number is calling. I signal for Nate to shut up as I answer the call and put it on speaker.

"Hello," I say.

"Jaxon, my man," comes the voice of Cole. "You're awake."

"Sure am, asshole. Now where is she?" I say, venom lacing my tone.

"Straight to business, huh?" he comments.

"Damn right."

"Now where would the fun in me telling you be?"

"Cole, I don't know why the fuck you are doing this, but Zoey has nothing to do with what went down." My jaw clenches as I struggle not to throw the phone in anger—the only lifeline I have to Zoey at this moment in time.

'Keep him talking,' Nate mouths as he quietly starts tapping buttons on his phone before placing it beside mine on the table to show a screen with a map on it and some other shit I can't make out.

"Doesn't she? I mean, you've been so focussed on finding her and having your fucking moment of vengeance that she's addled your brain, brother. You see, whilst you've been pining for the piece of pussy that got your brother killed, I've been building my own empire."

"The fuck are you talking about?" I bark.

"It doesn't always pay to trust those around you."

"Yeah, I got the memo."

"I don't think you have. You all saw me as the pathetic one, the man who couldn't keep his dick in his pants and didn't have the brain power to be at the top. Well, more fucking fool you, because I own this fucking town now. Not you, not Ronan, not Nate fucking Knowles… just me."

"Are you high? Because this all sounds rather delusional," I comment as Nate leans over the table and mouths 'Bingo' at me before he's moving quickly, striding from the room with me following behind, my phone in my hand as Cole continues to talk.

"You always wanted the name of the man at the top of the chain… well, you're talking to him," Cole says, and I nearly drop the damn phone from shock.

"What?"

"I've been running things for months, and right under your nose too," he says, and then he laughs. "It was easy because you were always distracted. And then when Zoey returned, well, it was like I had free fucking reign. That and the fact that she was the very thing I needed to fuck over every one of you that has looked down on me. Every bit of your time and focus was on her, and I bided my time and now she belongs to me."

"And you want her to screw with me?"

"Not just you. Ronan too. Nate not so much because I don't really know the guy, but if it makes people fear my name instead of his then it's a fucking bonus."

Nate storms out of the house, picking his car keys up as he goes, and I follow him to his car, still keeping Cole on the other end of the line.

The engine starts and Nate begins to drive like a bat out of hell, his phone in a holder as he follows his mark—the map on his phone, and I'm guessing it's a tracking app of some description and that he's got Cole's location.

"Cole, listen to me, you don't have to do this—"

"Oh I do, and I have. And in one hour, Zoey will just be another woman to become part of the trafficking ring. I've already got a buyer for her, and they are willing to pay a pretty hefty price for the sister of a crime lord, but don't worry, he's not the sickest of my clients. I mean, he's not far off, but he's not the worst."

"I'm going to fucking kill you," I say, my voice low—dangerous.

Cole laughs as Nate picks up even more speed. "I highly doubt that. I'm pretty sure you're tracing this call right now, but it'll be too late. Call it poetic justice, if you will, because the ending is where it all began."

"See you soon, asshole," I say before I cut the call and clench my jaw. I quickly dial Kev and tell him to put me on speakerphone so Shorty and whoever else is there can hear what I am about to tell them.

"Kev, have you found anything?" I say as soon as he picks up the call.

"No, and we've been to every one of our hideouts, his house, and contacted anyone that knows him."

"Fuck," I fume, and then I give him a very quick rundown of my conversation with Cole just now.

"What do you need us to do?" he asks.

"Go and meet Ronan at Purity, he'll direct you from there," Nate says before I can answer. It would normally be in me to argue but this is us working together.

"Jax?" Kev says in question.

"Do it."

"Okay, brother. We'll call if there's any news."

I cut the call and silence resumes. I rack my brains for any fucking place that he could be. I don't for one minute think he's at the location we're heading for. He's been a sneaky bastard, and he's had time to plan all of this. He wouldn't make it that easy to find him, not now.

We're wasting valuable time.

*Think, Jax, think.*

He's not at any of our hideouts. He's not at home. He's not with anyone that we know.

*"The ending is where it all began."*

*"The ending is where it all began."*

His final words play on repeat in my mind, and then I get a gut feeling that I can't shake.

"Turn around," I tell Nate.

"What?"

"Turn the car around."

"This is the only lead we have, Jax. I'm not about to turn around and throw away the chance to catch this bastard and find my sister," he rages.

"He's been planning this for months. He's not going to be where your fucking phone app says. Turn the damn car around and head for The Lodge."

The car screeches to a halt and Nate grinds his teeth.

We all know what happened at The Lodge the last time.

Torture. Death.

It changed all of our lives the last time, and if I'm right and he's there with her, then it will change our lives once again if we don't save her.

"Think with your head, Nate," I tell him. *"The ending is where it all began."*

"Shit," he says before he spins the car around and heads back in the direction we've just come from.

I bring Kev's number back up as Nate dials Ronan, and we each tell them where we're headed and to send back up. And if she isn't there, then I fear Cole is telling the truth and we really will be out of time.

# Chapter Twenty-Eight

## Zoey

I hate this place.

So many lives lost. So much pain. And now, here I am, back at The Lodge, and yet again I'm here with a sadistic fucker.

The last time was with Jessica and Lucas—my brother. And now it's with Cole, who appears to be running this whole operation—trafficking women.

My body trembles from the cold. Not surprising really seeing as I'm dressed in nothing but a pair of knickers and a bra. I was stripped of my shirt and Jax's boxers the minute I regained consciousness and had a gun held to my head so I would put the matching lingerie on. Then I was chained to the wall, in the exact room where I killed Jessica and where Nate took out our brother.

I feel like I'm about to throw up any minute now.

The memories. The flashbacks. They're invading my mind and making me weak.

Cole has done his fucking research, and now he's going to use my pain to break me—and the people I love.

I never should have come back. I could have taken punishment from Jax—hell, I almost let him take my life. But taking this punishment from Cole, a guy I never really fucking knew... I am not on board.

"It's nothing personal," he says from across the other side of the room where he sits behind a table with his feet on top of it, puffing on a cigar as if he is the ruler of the fucking world. "It was just too good an opportunity to pass up when you came back and I saw the hold you had over Jaxon without even knowing it. Like the cherry on top of the cake.

"And then there's Ronan, thinking he can order me about like I'm his little lap dog."

I haven't spoken a word to him. There's no point trying to reason with crazy—been there, done that, and it never works.

"They all thought they had me by the balls. Well, I showed them. Never underestimate the underdog."

The two guys guarding the door look bored to death. I suppose if they have to listen to this bullshit day in and day out then I guess I can't really blame them.

How the hell has Cole been allowed to have this much power? How has he slipped through the net of the most ruthless motherfuckers to walk the streets? Would this have happened if Nate had been around? Probably not. But then again, I can't presume anything. Nate has changed since he's been with Kat and become a father. His bad side has been locked away for years, and I would hate to be the reason that it came back out.

I am always the cause. Me. It's always me at the root of everyone's problems.

Maybe this is for the best?

Maybe they'll all be better off without me?

The thought makes me want to bawl my eyes out, but I won't give this asshat the satisfaction of seeing me crumble so quickly—on the outside, at least.

"You know, they were looking for the top guy for so long. It's fucking funny that not one of them considered me to be a threat. And then Jax thought he could oust me, as if he's some sort of God who can play with people's lives. Laughable really," he continues.

I wish he'd shut the fuck up and let me wallow in peace.

The cuffs around my wrists are digging in, and my arms are aching from being held above my head for fuck knows how long.

"Only half an hour to go and then your new owner will be whisking you away to pastures new," Cole says, and I shudder. "But don't worry, he's not the worst of my clients. I mean, I'm sure he'll inflict pain and suffering as he sees fit, but you'll enjoy it. They all enjoy it eventually." He's beyond crazy. Totally bat shit.

"And the best part is that Jax will be stupid enough to trace my call and end up in the wrong place. It's truly marvellous what technology can do—pinging my mobile phone reception to a different location altogether. And by the time he realises his mistake, you'll be long gone, and I'll be the one calling all the shots. Those fuckers will work for me. I'll own their asses, and they'll wish they had never crossed me."

I can do nothing but watch Cole believe that he will win this war. I won't even try to tell him that he can't, because once

Nate gets hold of him, he'll be a dead man. Seems I will be the reason that Nate reverts to his old self after all.

I always thought I was strong, but really, I've been kidding myself.

I'm broken, bound and chained up like an animal.

"Fifteen minutes, boss," a voice says from behind the burly men blocking the door.

"Boss… doesn't that sound magnificent?" Cole asks, but no one answers. "Well, I guess I better go down and get ready to greet your new owner." Cole gets up and buttons up the suit jacket he's wearing as he walks around the table and comes to stand in front of me.

"Oh, and the guy you left on Jaxon's kitchen floor, you know, with his Achilles cut, nice move," he says with a wink. "It's been a pleasure, Zoey Knowles." He throws me an evil smirk before turning and leaving the room, the guard dogs moving out of his way for him to pass before they block the doorway again.

So, I guess this is where my story ends.

At The Lodge.

Being sold to a guy who will probably torture me before deciding he needs a new plaything and killing me.

I almost laugh at how ridiculous this is, like a warped tale of a lost girl who just wanted to make peace with her sins and find love.

Except… I'm not lost.

Since being back here, even with all the shit that's been thrown my way, I'm home.

I'm not lost, not anymore.

Jax. He's my home, and I'll be fucking damned if Cole takes that away from me.

I've been taught by the best in the business. I've killed

people. I've always been a fighter, minus the last few years where I've been a miserable pain in the ass, of course.

I can get out of here.

I can do it.

I have no idea how, but I can't just give up.

This isn't how I want to go out.

And with a renewed sense of purpose, I look for any little sign of how I can get out of here on my own, and not with someone coming to save my ass.

## Chapter Twenty-Nine

### Jax

We don't even bother to park away and walk on foot as we screech down the road for The Lodge. We're going in, all guns blazing. We've had no time to plan, but we're good at what we do, and even with just the two of us to start with, we'll be able to take the fuckers by surprise.

Nate floors it as we turn into the compound of The Lodge, and we race up to the building, screeching to a stop as close to the front door as possible. We don't waste any time as we both get out of the car, guns raised, game faces on.

This might be the stupidest fucking idea ever, but we're both here for Zoey, and we'll fight whoever gets in the way. Two guys at the front door jump back in shock, and it's long enough for Nate to sink a bullet in one as I take out the other.

He signals for me to go right, and he goes left as we enter the building. I'm amazed to see that there isn't anyone else stood in here, but that's okay because we'll kill them all when they show their faces.

My adrenaline pumps, my senses on high alert as I hear the sound of feet approaching me, pounding along the floor. Stupid fucks clearly didn't take a lesson in how to sneak up on the enemy. I duck into a doorway, checking the room quickly before turning back to face whoever is about to come into view.

Three.

Two.

One.

I step out as they appear, and I quickly hit my mark. The first guy gets a bullet straight between the eyes, and the other right in the mouth, each one dropping to the floor like sacks of shit. I quickly move over them and to the stairs. My gut is telling me she's up there. She has to be.

I hear shots ring out in the direction Nate went, but I have to believe that he can handle it as I hear a scream from upstairs and I launch myself into action, taking the steps three at a time.

Please let her be okay.

Please, please, please.

I come to a long hallway, and I race down it, thanking fuck that the doors that line either side are all closed. Saves me the job of having to try and sweep each room before I get to her. Another scream comes from the end of the hallway, and I pump my legs harder, my biker boots pounding on the floor as I go.

I bring my gun up in front of me, ready to fire as I hear Zoey shout, "Fucking die, asshole."

Huh?

I am about to turn into the room with the only open door when a body smacks into me.

"Oof." I'm momentarily knocked back a bit, but I manage to wrap my arms around the body that smacked into me. A body I know well. A body that appears to not be wearing any clothes other than some lingerie. What the fuck?

"Zoey."

"Jax," she says as I help steady her, her eyes wide with a wild look in them. "We have to get out of here... he's coming, he's going to take me, I need to get out..." She's rambling, not making any sense, but she can explain when I get her to safety. I quickly move her to the side and peer into the room she just came out of to see a guy dead on the floor, his head bashed in and blood pooling all around him.

"Did you do that?" I ask Zoey as I turn back to look at her, taking in the blood that splatters her bare skin.

She nods and then she's urging me to move. Well fuck.

I push myself in front of her, taking her hand in mine and leading her down the hallway and to the stairs. I'd like to get some fucking clothes on her, but I don't have time to look for any right now, so I quickly take off my jumper and give it to her. She doesn't waste any time in putting it on and I peer over the side and see several men below, so I open fire on them, taking out three before I have to duck because one of the bastards takes a shot back at me.

I keep Zoey behind me, and then I hear the roar of bikes out the front. About fucking time. I know that shit is about to get a whole lot worse, and I need to get her out of here.

I move up and peer over the side again to see Kev, Shorty and Gator come running in, followed by some of Nate's guys.

"Okay, get ready to go," I tell her, and I feel her squeeze my hand a little harder.

"Not so fast, Jaxon."

Fucking Cole.

I turn around slowly to see he has gun pointed at me, and another in his other hand pointed at Zoey. "Drop the gun and get up."

I want to argue with him, I want to tell him that I'm going to rip his fucking throat out and shove it up his ass, but it'll have to wait for now as I feel Zoey gently squeeze my hand once before she starts to rise. I'm aware that if we stand, we will be in sight of the men down below, but I have to hope that no one takes a shot at us. I reluctantly place the gun by my foot before I stand up.

"Kick it away," Cole instructs, and I flick the gun away with my foot. "So, it seems you've brought chaos to my headquarters."

"Your headquarters?" I question.

"Been here for months and no one had any idea," he tells me with a laugh. "All those nights you thought I'd gone home to cry over Shanice, and really, I was here, planning your demise."

"My demise?"

"You've always looked down your fucking nose at me," Cole snarls. "Always thought you were better than everyone. It's just a shame that Jason died instead of you." I feel Zoey clamp her other hand on my arm to make sure I don't lose it and get us both killed.

"Interesting," Cole says as his eyes drop to Zoey's hand on my arm, and then our linked fingers. "So, I guess you like to keep it in the family, huh?"

"I swear to God—"

"What?" He cuts me off. "What are you going to fucking

do? I could take you both out right now and there isn't anything you can do about it."

I don't think I've ever hated someone as much as I hate Cole right now. And it just shows me that I never truly hated Zoey, not even a little bit. My frustration and stubborn ass tried to tell me that I did, but deep down, I know now that I didn't.

"Give her to me," he demands, but I step in front of her, keeping my body shielding hers.

"Not gonna happen."

"I've got a client who is coming to collect her, and I am going to deliver," he tells me, but I curl my lip back in disgust.

"Over my dead body," I snarl, and then the shot rings out.

I hear Zoey shout out but it's like time stops as I feel her push me from the side. I lose my footing and stumble to the floor, Zoey falling on top of me. Her hands are searching everywhere, my chest, my arms, my face. Her eyes are darting over me, but all I can really think about is the fact that she pushed me out of the way.

"I'm okay," I tell her as I grab her wrists and hold them in place to stop her from trying to find a bullet wound. There isn't one, not on me anyway. I turn my head to the side and see Cole is lying dead on the floor, his eyes still open, his mouth wide with shock, and then I look up to see Nate stood behind him, the gun still pointing in front of him.

"Get her out of here," he barks at me, and I'm up and on my feet as quick as lightening. There's still the sound of fighting downstairs, but then Nate says, "I'll cover you. Go."

I pick Zoey up, moving her legs so they hook around my waist, and then I run.

I run down towards the commotion, praying like fuck that I

get her out of here unharmed. I charge through the scene playing out around me, and I step over the bodies that are on the floor. Fuck, Cole really did have a team hidden away up here—unless they're any of Nate's guys, but I haven't got time to look too closely as I barrel through the front door and head for the first bike I see. With the keys still in the ignition, I thank my lucky stars that my guys had the sense to leave keys for anyone who needed to get away quickly. We don't ever worry about people stealing our shit, because anyone that has tried has always been found and dealt with pretty damn quick—and word spreads.

I hook my leg over the bike, starting it up, keeping Zoey attached to my front, and then I'm racing us away, leaving all the chaos behind us as she clings to me, her legs and arms wrapped around me as we escape from a place that holds nothing but nightmares.

# Chapter Thirty

## Zoey

I cling on to Jax for dear life as he navigates us fuck knows where. I don't even care right now, just so long as we're away from The Lodge. I wish Nate were with us too, but I know he won't leave there until every last person who sided with Cole is dead. I pray that he will be okay, I didn't even get to say anything to him before he told Jax to get me out of there, and then my ass was being hauled away.

If anything happens to my brother, I swear to God, I'll lose it. He only came back here because of me. Him and Kat were living in paradise with Gracie, and I'm the reason he's in the middle of all this shit going down now.

My face is buried in Jax's chest when I feel the bike come to a stop, and then he's lifting me with him off of the bike. I look to the side to see that we've stopped outside a large building that looks like a warehouse in the middle of nowhere, and I utter the first words since we left The Lodge. "Is it safe here?"

"It's safe, pretty girl."

Pretty girl. I never thought I would grow to like him calling me that, but actually, now it would feel strange if he didn't call me it. Funny how things change so quickly, and how life can put things in perspective when you least expect it.

A few weeks ago, Jax was my enemy. And now, I couldn't imagine him not being in my life.

But where do we go from here?

"Jax," I say softly as he carries me towards the front door and keys in a code on a panel to the side to unlock it. When we enter, dim lights come on automatically, and I am pleasantly surprised to see that it might look like a shitty warehouse on the outside, but on the inside, it's decked out rather nicely. Jax walks me through a large open-plan kitchen and dining area, through a hallway which has a couple of doors lined either side, and then he's taking me into a room at the end, which is a bathroom, stopping beside a walk-in shower.

"We'll talk later, but right now, you need to get warm," he tells me as he reaches over and turns on the shower before moving his hands to the hem of the jumper I'm wearing and pulling it up and over my head. Next, he twirls his finger for me to turn around, and then he undoes the bra and I let it fall to the floor. And then he crouches down behind me and removes the knickers before guiding me in the shower. He goes to turn away from me, but I put my hand on his arm and say, "Please don't leave me on my own."

I realise I probably sound pathetic, but I need to feel him. I need him close. I don't know what happens after this, and if this is my last moment with him, then I'm not about to waste it. Especially when we both came so close to being killed.

His lips lock with mine and he gets in without even bothering to take his clothes off. I don't mind, I'm happy to undress him. I take my time removing his clothes, and when I do, Jax doesn't even bother to kick them out of the shower and just leaves them to the side of our feet.

He caresses my body, feeling every inch of my skin, almost as if he can't believe that I'm here.

And when he lifts me and slides inside of me, it reminds me that I'm home.

---

We're sitting at the kitchen table, Jax holding my hand as he sits opposite me and an untouched cup of coffee sat in front of me, when my phone rings.

I snatch it off of the table and see Kat's name lighting up the screen.

"Kat," I say as I answer.

"He's okay," she says, not even bothering with saying anything else because she'll know that I've been waiting to be told that my brother is safe.

"Oh thank God," I say as I breathe a sigh of relief. "Is he there?"

"No, not yet. He just phoned to say he's dealing with the buyer and that he'll be back when he's done."

"Oh, Kat, I am so sorry," I say as tears start to fall down my cheeks.

"Stop that right now. You have no need to apologise."

"Yes, I do."

"No," she says firmly. "You didn't come back here and expect to be fucking kidnapped by a nut job. You came back to appease the guilt that has plagued you for years, and I swear to

God, if you let this eat you up as well, then I am seriously going to kick your ass."

I can't help it as I laugh through my tears.

"You're pregnant, Kat," I say.

"What does that matter? Just means you can't stop me," she says. I love my sister-in-law. She's the best thing that ever happened to my brother, and to me. She loves me no matter what, and the feeling is mutual.

"Can you get Nate to call me when he gets home?" I ask.

"No. I'll get him to call you in the morning. He told me you're with Jax, and I know for damn sure that you're gonna need tonight to just be about the two of you before your brother starts issuing ultimatums and threatening to cut Jax's dick off if he hurts you, blah blah blah," she says with sarcasm, and again, I'm laughing.

"I love you, Kat," I tell her.

"Love you too, sis," she replies before she cuts the call.

"Nate's okay," I say to Jax, even though he's just heard my side of the conversation and it doesn't take a rocket scientist to figure it out.

"I figured. And, uh, Kat, she seems…"

"Like she can hold her own?"

"I was going to go with she seems like she doesn't take any shit, but sure, hold your own works too," he says.

"Yeah, she's the best," I say with a smile.

"It's good to see you smile like that." And even though this guy has had his face buried in my pussy more than once, I feel myself blush at the compliment.

"Kat's right though," he continues, and I look at him in question. "We need to figure shit out before he *tries* to threaten to cut my dick off."

I chuckle at him, and he smiles. This is nice, easy, something we haven't had between us yet. Our relationship is complicated and has been full of fucking tension, so it's a welcome change to have it feel... simple, even for just a moment.

"We have so much history, Jax..." My voice trails off because if we're going to get into it, where the fuck are we supposed to start? We've spoken before, but this feels like it could make or break us, and I really don't want it to be the latter.

"We do, but living in the past has done neither of us any favours," Jax starts. "We've both been punished enough. If we keep thinking that we need to punish ourselves, then we're never really going to live."

I nod my head at him as I try to find the words I need to say, but then he speaks again.

"I am so fucking sorry for what I have done to you, Zoey. I'm ashamed of my actions, and I allowed my grief and pain to turn me into a monster."

"You're not a monster, Jax."

"No? So what would you call a guy who arranged to have you kidnapped and taken to a house so he could break you? A guy who put his hands around your throat and nearly took your life... is that not a monster?"

His eyes, they are showing me everything in this moment. Sorrow. Remorse. Shame. Guilt. Despair. Longing. It's all there as he finally opens up his heart to me.

"I hurt you. I was going to fucking kill you, and I don't know how to live with those choices," he continues, and I feel a lump form in my throat. "I don't know how I can ever show you just how sorry I truly am."

"I don't need you to show me, because you already have," I tell him honestly. "You came for me. You were prepared to die for me back at The Lodge. You stood in front of me—"

"Until you shoved me," he grumbles, cutting me off, and I can't stop the chuckle that leaves me.

"It was instinct," I say as I roll my eyes.

"But it's my job to protect you," he says, and the amusement from seconds ago disappears as he holds my gaze. "And I finally understand why Jason did what he did."

"How do you mean?" I ask quietly as I wait with bated breath to see what he says.

"I understand why he went, why he chose to go with you. When I realised you'd been taken, I knew I'd kill to get you back. I knew that I wouldn't have stopped until I found you. I finally understand that when you love someone, you'll do anything for them."

My hand comes to my mouth as I process what he just said.

*'When you love someone, you'll do anything for them.'*

"Because I do love you, pretty girl. The way you make me crazy with every emotion possible, the way you invade my mind, the way that you've brought me back to life…" He closes his eyes briefly and I feel my heart rate pick up as it pounds against my chest.

"Jax…"

"It's always been you," he whispers, and I get up and move around the table to go to him. He moves back slightly, and I straddle his lap, cupping his face in my hands.

"You better mean everything you're saying, Jax Jones," I tell him.

"Every fucking word," he replies, no hesitation.

And I feel something I haven't felt in a long time surge

through me. Pure fucking happiness. That's it. Just happiness and love for the crazy bastard in front of me.

"I love you too, Jax," I tell him, but he looks at me like I'm not making any sense.

"Even after everything I've done to you?" he questions.

"Yes, because what we have is crazy stupid love. It's unique and it's ours," I answer and bring my lips to his.

"Crazy stupid love," he says against my lips, and I can feel the smile that spreads across his face. "I like that."

"That's us, biker boy," I say before our lips crash together.

Love makes you do crazy things, and loving Jax will be one hell of a ride, but we've battled through all the ugliness to find the beauty. It hasn't been easy, and I have no doubt that we'll clash over many things in the future, but I'll clash with him every single time if it means I get to keep his heart.

As far as I'm concerned, this is when we start to live again. With each other. And together, we can get through anything.

## Chapter Thirty-One

### Jax

To say the last couple of weeks has been eventful would be an understatement, but it's shown me that life doesn't always work out the way you planned.

I never expected for my brother to die young.

I never expected to have one of my men betray me.

I never expected to fall in love with a woman I convinced myself I hated.

And I never expected to be shaking hands with a crime lord as I stand before Nate Knowles and promise to protect his sister at all fucking costs.

We've had the talk, he's promised to end my life if I ever so much as hurt a hair on her head from here on out, and in turn, he's promised to give me a chance, despite the past.

He loves his sister, and so do I, and ultimately, that's all that fucking matters.

Zoey is stood next to me, and I put my arm around her

shoulders, pulling her to my side as she has a smile on her face that should never have been absent.

I plan to spend the rest of my days making up for all of my wrongs, and after eating her pussy for the last week, I'm pretty sure I've got that particular part down pat.

She's told me I don't have to make up for anything, but I absolutely do. And I will. She will be the only one to ever truly see the real me, and even with all of my darkness, she still loves me.

Love.

Fuck.

Never thought I'd see the day. And I know that my brother wouldn't hold a grudge. He would want me to be happy—Zoey too.

It'll take time to put the nightmare of what Cole did behind us, but with all of his associates dead, there will be no reminders other than our own memories, which will hopefully fade over time.

We've lost so much time already, and I refuse to lose anymore.

My life starts here, with Zoey, together.

Crazy stupid love, and I wouldn't have it any other way.

## Chapter Thirty-Two

### Zoey

There is a side to Jaxon Jones that not many people see.

There is a man who finds it hard to let people in.

There is a man that loves so hard but reserves it for very few.

To look at Jax, you see he's a big, strong, mysterious and handsome man who would rather scowl at you than smile… but once you crack your way past his walls of steel, you'll see that he has a big heart, and his loyalty holds no bounds.

We have had one hell of a journey. We've both experienced pain, hurt, suffering, longing for something that neither of us realised we needed… each other.

I know that I loved Jason, but not like I love Jax. I am madly in love with the biker brut who drives me crazy daily, but even when he pisses me off it's in the best way.

The emotions I've experienced since returning home have made me come alive again.

I plan to laugh, to joke, and to enjoy every single moment, unlike before when I was just floating along and putting on a face that I wanted everyone to see.

And I'm going to do all of that with Jax.

My life.

My heart.

My home.

## Chapter Thirty-Three

### Ronan

"Earth to Ronan, come in Ronan," I hear as a hand is thrust in front of my face, blocking the computer screen from my view.

"What?" I snap as I look up to see Zoey stood there, her hands going to her hips as she looks at me. "Sorry," I say as I run my hand over my face.

"You need to take a fucking break," she says, but I scoff in response.

"I can't take a break, Zoey," I tell her as I groan at the pile of paperwork I still have to go through.

"You do know that I am back now and that I can take care of some of this," she tells me as she points to the paperwork that sits on the desk like it's fucking taunting me. I hate paperwork. So fucking boring. And I could have let someone else run Purity, but I never truly felt like I could let it go.

"I know, but I've been doing it for so long, it's just habit," I say.

"Okay, so let me put it another way… fuck off and get a drink and then tomorrow you can catch me up to speed and we can work out a new system. It is my club after all, Ronan," Zoey says, but not in a shitty way, I know she's just trying to lighten my load.

Nate is going back home tomorrow, and I'm going to miss that fucker being around. Been nice having him back, even if that does sound girlie as shit.

"Fine," I say with a sigh as I stand up and push the chair back before I round the desk. "Good to have you back in the driving seat, Zozo," I say, ruffling her hair as I walk past.

"Hey," she says, and I chuckle as I make my way through the corridor, past the VIP section, and into the main bar.

The place isn't open yet, and I find myself alone in the bar with Kayla. Fucking Kayla. God she gets right up my nose. She hears the door close behind me and looks up, giving me an eye roll and a scowl when she sees its me.

Warm greeting as always.

"Vodka, straight up," I tell her as I take a seat at the bar.

"Get it yourself," she retorts, bending down to place some bottles on a lower shelf. She might be infuriating, but fuck, her ass is something to be desired. Round and peachy, just how I like. Shame about her mouth.

"You're the bar staff," I say, knowing it will piss her off further.

"And I'm not on the clock yet."

"So why are you here already then?" Kayla is always early. I can't even recall a time when she missed a shift or turned up late. She's a model employee, except for the bad attitude towards me.

"Fuck off, Ronan. Zoey is back now, so do us both a favour and leave me alone," she sasses, and I am up and off my stool so fucking fast, rounding the bar and caging her in as I place my arms either side of her, my palms resting on the bar top.

"Watch how you speak to me, Kayla," I warn, but she doesn't look phased in the slightest.

"Why? Is the big, scary bad man going to threaten me into submission?" she retorts, and fuck if the word submission doesn't have my dick stirring.

"I get that you have a problem with me, but don't for one minute think that I wouldn't fire your ass and send you on your merry way," I tell her, staring her down, her light blue coloured eyes glowing with defiance.

"Considering I haven't been able to stand you for the last six years, and I've made it very obvious, why haven't you already fired me?" she asks with a smirk.

The fucking minx.

"Seems I like to keep my enemies close," I respond.

"Is that so?" she says as she brings her hand up and places a finger on my chest before she runs it slowly down my front. "I guess that one time I lost my mind holds a place in your heart, huh?"

She's referring to the time that we fucked. In this bar. After closing hours, when everyone had gone home. I've tried to block that from my mind since it happened, because goddamn can this woman get under my skin without adding another dimension to our relationship—if you can call it that.

I struggle to think why she started hating me in the first place as her lips hover inches from mine.

"Just because my dick liked you once upon a time doesn't mean that I do," I say, and just like that, the spell we were both under for a few seconds there disappears.

"That's right, because all Ronan Pierce cares about is getting his own way and to hell with everyone else."

"Damn straight." I don't even deny it. I'm a selfish fuck and I own it.

"One day you'll come unstuck, and when you do, I'll be there, watching as your world crumbles around you." And with that, she ducks down, brushing against my front as she moves under my arm and rounds the bar, disappearing through the main doors and out of sight.

Fuck.

That woman would be the death of me if I let her, and I have no intention of letting that happen.

## Chapter Thirty-Four

### Nate

"You really want to do this?" I ask Kat as she looks at me with that mischievous glint in her eyes.

"I sure do," she says with a smile.

"But we'd be giving up our idyllic life for all of the chaos," I tell her, needing her to be sure that this is really what she wants.

She saunters towards me, her hips swaying, her tiny baby bump just starting to show. Fuck, she is a goddess. My goddess. So fucking thankful I gave her that ultimatum all those years ago.

"Chaos can be fun," she says as she places her hands on my chest and looks up at me.

"And what about Gracie and the baby?" I ask her.

"You don't think you can protect them?"

"Don't ask me stupid fucking questions, wife," I tell her. I can protect my family better than anyone else I know. No fucker will be getting within a mile of them if we do this.

She smirks but then turns serious. "You miss it," she says, not even asking it but stating a fact. My wife knows me better than anyone, and she is the only person in the world that I would let read me in this way.

"But I love you, Gracie and the baby more," I tell her truthfully.

"I know," she says, and I lean down and rest my forehead on hers. "But we've had five years, and it's been amazing, don't get me wrong, but I know you, Nate. I know that you miss the adrenaline, the chase, the control. And I know that the kids and I will be just as happy here."

"I fucking love you," I growl at her as I crash my lips to hers.

Her hands link behind my neck as I devour her. I will never get my fill of her.

And when she breaks her lips from mine, she says, "Make me fucking scream, husband."

I smirk at her and let her go before I tell her, "Five second head start, baby, make it count."

She giggles, actually fucking giggles and runs off as I count down from five.

My wife just agreed that we could stay. Here. In our home. The place where we fell in love and where I ruled the streets.

And as I finish the countdown and chase after her, I can't help but think how fucking good it is to be back.

## THE END

# Acknowledgments

And there we have it. Zoey and Jax got their story, and as you can see, I am not done with this world yet… *winky face*

Ronan and Kayla will be getting their story.

Kat and Nate may get another book because I am obsessed with the crime lord and his sassy wife.

I would like to thank my other half for supporting me and for doing all the things when I'm chained to my desk, lol.

I would like to thank my betas, Nikki, Farrell and Lyndsey for settling my doubts and for always being there when I'm having a moment.

I would like to thank my street team and ARC team for being so bloody awesome! You guys rock!

To my readers, without you, I wouldn't even be at this point. Thank you for reading my words, for loving my characters and for continuing to remind me why I do this.

And now, on to the next one…

Much love,
    Lindsey.

# Wrecking Ball

Have you met the Crime Lord yet?
It's where it all started…
Keep reading for the first chapter…

SHE HAS TO BE
SMART TO GET
OUT ALIVE...

# WRECKING
*Ball*

## A FORCED MARRIAGE DARK ROMANCE

# LINDSEY POWELL

## Chapter One

### Kat

Every girl dreams about it.

Every woman plans it.

The white dress.

The pretty flowers.

The handsome man waiting at the altar.

And that is the most important part.

The guy. The one you want to spend the rest of your life with. The one that will cherish you, love you, protect you and make you feel like they would move heaven and earth to make you happy.

Yeah. That guy.

Except, I'm not marrying that guy.

Instead, I'm stood next to the devil with a fake smile plastered on my face.

I'm wearing the dress and I have the pretty flowers, but that's as far as it goes. The rest has all been fabricated.

You see, I'm stood here because of a debt. A debt I stupidly thought I could repay with money, but no. Instead, I'm paying with my life, and it's all my fault.

I lost and gambled away my own future.

Crazy, huh?

That it may be, but it's happened and here I am.

I'm not marrying the man I love; I'm marrying the most dangerous guy in the country.

Nate Knowles.

Number one asshole and blackmail extraordinaire.

I had a debt with the most powerful man in the crime world, and I truly believed that I could have paid him back… until I didn't.

One wrong choice was my downfall.

And that choice I made was for love. A love that turned out to be false. The man I thought I loved turned his back on me and left me to rot.

And now, here I am.

Bowing down to the crime lord where his world involves popping a bullet in someone's head as if it is as normal as eating breakfast.

Playing ball is what will keep me alive.

Acting the part is what will stop me from being fifty feet under.

So, even as I hate Nate Knowles with a passion, I will smile and say the right things in public, but in private, all bets are off.

I need a plan, a way to get the hell out of this nightmare.

I need to suss things out, ingrain myself so deep that he will never see it coming.

Role of a lifetime.

Good meets evil.
And I will take down the monster.
You just see if I don't…

## About the Author

Lindsey lives in South West, England, with her partner and two children. She works within a family run business, and she began her writing career in 2013. She finds the time to write in-between working and raising a family.

Lindsey's love of reading inspired her to create her own book series. Her favourite book genre is romance, but her interests span over several genre's including mystery, suspense and crime.

To keep up to date with book news, you can find Lindsey on social media and you can also check out Lindsey's website where you can find all of her books and her newsletter:

https://lindseypowellauthor.wordpress.com

- facebook.com/lindseypowellperfect
- twitter.com/Lindsey_perfect
- instagram.com/lindseypowellperfect
- bookbub.com/authors/lindsey-powell
- goodreads.com/lpow21
- tiktok.com/@lpowperfect

Printed in Great Britain
by Amazon